COBWEBS

FROM AN EMPTY SKULL

Ambrose Bierce
(AKA: Dod Grile)

Cobwebs From an Empty Skull

Ambrose Bierce (AKA: Dod Grile)

© 1st World Library, 2006
PO Box 2211
Fairfield, IA 52556
www.1stworldlibrary.com
First Edition

LCCN: 2006936182

Softcover ISBN: 978-1-4218-3020-9
Hardcover ISBN: 978-1-4218-2920-3
eBook ISBN: 978-1-4218-3120-6

Purchase *"Cobwebs From an Empty Skull"*
as a traditional bound book at:
www.1stWorldLibrary.com/purchase.asp?ISBN=978-1-4218-3020-9

1st World Library is a literary, educational organization
dedicated to:

- Creating a free internet library of downloadable ebooks

- Hosting writing competitions and offering book
publishing scholarships.

Interested in more 1st World Library books?
contact: literacy@1stworldlibrary.com
Check us out at: www.1stworldlibrary.com

1st World Library Literary Society

Giving Back to the World

"If you want to work on the core problem, it's early school literacy."

- James Barksdale, former CEO of Netscape

"No skill is more crucial to the future of a child, or to a democratic and prosperous society, than literacy."

- Los Angeles Times

Literacy... means far more than learning how to read and write... The aim is to transmit... knowledge and promote social participation."

- UNESCO

"Literacy is not a luxury, it is a right and a responsibility. If our world is to meet the challenges of the twenty-first century we must harness the energy and creativity of all our citizens."

- President Bill Clinton

"Parents should be encouraged to read to their children, and teachers should be equipped with all available techniques for teaching literacy, so the varying needs and capacities of individual kids can be taken into account."

- Hugh Mackay

To my friend,

SHERBURNE B. EATON

CONTENTS

PREFACE

The matter of which this volume is composed appeared originally in the columns of "FUN," when the wisdom of the Fables and the truth of the Tales tended to wholesomely diminish the levity of that jocund sheet. Their publication in a new form would seem to be a fitting occasion to say something as to their merit.

Homer's "Iliad," it will be remembered, was but imperfectly appreciated by Homer's contemporaries. Milton's "Paradise Lost" was so lightly regarded when first written, that the author received but twenty-five pounds for it. Ben Jonson was for some time blind to the beauties of Shakespeare, and Shakespeare himself had but small esteem for his own work.

Appearing each week in "FUN," these Fables and Tales very soon attracted the notice of the Editor, who was frank enough to say, afterward, that when he accepted the manuscript he did not quite perceive the quality of it. The printers, too, into whose hands it came, have since admitted that for some days they felt very little interest in it, and could not even make out what it was all about. When to these evidences I add the confession that at first I did not myself observe anything extraordinary in my work, I think I need say no more: the discerning public will note the parallel, and my modesty be spared the necessity of making an ass of itself.

D.G.

FABLES OF ZAMBRI, THE PARSEE

I

A certain Persian nobleman obtained from a cow gipsy a small oyster. Holding him up by the beard, he addressed him thus:

"You must try to forgive me for what I am about to do; and you might as well set about it at once, for you haven't much time. I should never think of swallowing you if it were not so easy; but opportunity is the strongest of all temptations. Besides, I am an orphan, and very hungry."

"Very well," replied the oyster; "it affords me genuine pleasure to comfort the parentless and the starving. I have already done my best for our friend here, of whom you purchased me; but although she has an amiable and accommodating stomach, *we couldn't agree.* For this trifling incompatibility—would you believe it?—she was about to stew me! Saviour, benefactor, proceed."

"I think," said the nobleman, rising and laying down the oyster, "I ought to know something more definite about your antecedents before succouring you. If you couldn't agree with your mistress, you are probably no better than you should be."

People who begin doing something from a selfish motive frequently drop it when they learn that it is a real benevolence.

II

A rat seeing a cat approaching, and finding no avenue of escape, went boldly up to her, and said:

"Madam, I have just swallowed a dose of powerful bane, and in accordance with instructions upon the label, have come out of my hole to die. Will you kindly direct me to a spot where my corpse will prove peculiarly offensive?"

"Since you are so ill," replied the cat, "I will myself transport you to a spot which I think will suit."

So saying, she struck her teeth through the nape of his neck and trotted away with him. This was more than he had bargained for, and he squeaked shrilly with the pain.

"Ah!" said the cat, "a rat who knows he has but a few minutes to live, never makes a fuss about a little agony. I don't think, my fine fellow, you have taken poison enough to hurt either you or me."

So she made a meal of him.

If this fable does not teach that a rat gets no profit by lying, I should be pleased to know what it does teach.

Ambrose Bierce

III

A frog who had been sitting up all night in neighbourly converse with an echo of elegant leisure, went out in the grey of the morning to obtain a cheap breakfast. Seeing a tadpole approach,

"Halt!" he croaked, "and show cause why I should not eat you."

The tadpole stopped and displayed a fine tail.

"Enough," said the frog: "I mistook you for one of us; and if there is anything I like, it is frog. But no frog has a tail, as a matter of course."

While he was speaking, however, the tail ripened and dropped off, and its owner stood revealed in his edible character.

"Aha!" ejaculated the frog, "so that is your little game! If, instead of adopting a disguise, you had trusted to my mercy, I should have spared you. But I am down upon all manner of deceit."

And he had him down in a moment.

Learn from this that he would have eaten him anyhow.

IV

An old man carrying, for no obvious reason, a sheaf of sticks, met another donkey whose cargo consisted merely of a bundle of stones.

"Suppose we swop," said the donkey.

"Very good, sir," assented the old man; "lay your load upon my shoulders, and take off my parcel, putting it upon your own back."

The donkey complied, so far as concerned his own encumbrance, but neglected to remove that of the other.

"How clever!" said the merry old gentleman, "I knew you would do that. If you had done any differently there would have been no point to the fable."

And laying down both burdens by the roadside, he trudged away as merry as anything.

V

An elephant meeting a mouse, reproached him for not taking a proper interest in growth.

"It is all very well," retorted the mouse, "for people who haven't the capacity for anything better. Let them grow if they like; but *I* prefer toasted cheese."

The stupid elephant, not being able to make very much sense of this remark, essayed, after the manner of persons worsted at repartee, to set his foot upon his clever conqueror. In point of fact, he did set his foot upon him, and there wasn't any more mouse.

The lesson imparted by this fable is open, palpable: mice and elephants look at things each after the manner of his kind; and when an elephant decides to occupy the standpoint of a mouse, it is unhealthy for the latter.

VI

A wolf was slaking his thirst at a stream, when a lamb left the side of his shepherd, came down the creek to the wolf, passed round him with considerable ostentation, and began drinking below.

"I beg you to observe," said the lamb, "that water does not commonly run uphill; and my sipping here cannot possibly defile the current where you are, even supposing my nose were no cleaner than yours, which it is. So you have not the flimsiest pretext for slaying me."

"I am not aware, sir," replied the wolf, "that I require a pretext for loving chops; it never occurred to me that one was necessary."

And he dined upon that lambkin with much apparent satisfaction.

This fable ought to convince any one that of two stories very similar one needs not necessarily be a plagiarism.

Ambrose Bierce

VII

An old gentleman sat down, one day, upon an acorn, and finding it a very comfortable seat, went soundly to sleep. The warmth of his body caused the acorn to germinate, and it grew so rapidly, that when the sleeper awoke he found himself sitting in the fork of an oak, sixty feet from the ground.

"Ah!" said he, "I am fond of having an extended view of any landscape which happens to please my fancy; but this one does not seem to possess that merit. I think I will go home."

It is easier to say go home than to go.

"Well, well!" he resumed, "if I cannot compel circumstances to my will, I can at least adapt my will to circumstances. I decide to remain. 'Life'—as a certain eminent philosopher in England wilt say, whenever there shall be an England to say it in—'is the definite combination of heterogeneous changes, both simultaneous and successive, in correspondence with external co-existences and sequences.' I have, fortunately, a few years of this before me yet; and I suppose I can permit my surroundings to alter me into anything I choose."

And he did; but what a choice!

I should say that the lesson hereby imparted is one of contentment combined with science.

VIII

A caterpillar had crawled painfully to the top of a hop-pole, and not finding anything there to interest him, began to think of descending. "Now," soliloquized he, "if I only had a pair of wings, I should be able to manage it very nicely."

So saying, he turned himself about to go down, but the heat of his previous exertion, and that of the sun, had by this time matured him into a butterfly.

"Just my luck!" he growled, "I never wish for anything without getting it. I did not expect this when I came out this morning, and have nothing prepared. But I suppose I shall have to stand it."

So he spread his pinions and made for the first open flower he saw. But a spider happened to be spending the summer in that vegetable, and it was not long before Mr. Butterfly was wishing himself back atop of that pole, a simple caterpillar.

He had at last the pleasure of being denied a desire.

Haec fabula docet that it is not a good plan to call at houses without first ascertaining who is at home there.

Ambrose Bierce

IX

It is related of a certain Tartar priest that, being about to
sacrifice a pig, he observed tears in the victim's eyes.

"Now, I'd like to know what is the matter with *you*?" he asked.

"Sir," replied the pig, "if your penetration were equal to that of
the knife you hold, you would know without inquiring; but I
don't mind telling you. I weep because I know I shall be badly
roasted."

"Ah," returned the priest, meditatively, having first killed the
pig, "we are all pretty much alike: it is the bad roasting that
frightens us. Mere death has no terrors."

From this narrative learn that even priests sometimes get hold
of only half a truth.

X

A dog being very much annoyed by bees, ran, quite accident-ally, into an empty barrel lying on the ground, and looking out at the bung-hole, addressed his tormenters thus:

"Had you been temperate, stinging me only one at a time, you might have got a good deal of fun out of me. As it is, you have driven me into a secure retreat; for I can snap you up as fast as you come in through the bung-hole. Learn from this the folly of intemperate zeal."

When he had concluded, he awaited a reply. There wasn't any reply; for the bees had never gone near the bung-hole; they went in the same way as he did, and made it very warm for him.

The lesson of this fable is that one cannot stick to his pure reason while quarrelling with bees.

XI

A fox and a duck having quarrelled about the ownership of a frog, agreed to refer the dispute to a lion. After hearing a great deal of argument, the lion opened his mouth to speak.

"I am very well aware," interrupted the duck, "what your decision is. It is that by our own showing the frog belongs to neither of us, and you will eat him yourself. But please remember that lions do not like frogs."

"To me," exclaimed the fox, "it is perfectly clear that you will give the frog to the duck, the duck to me, and take me yourself. Allow me to state certain objections to—"

"I was about to remark," said the lion, "that while you were disputing, the cause of contention had hopped away. Perhaps you can procure another frog."

To point out the moral of this fable would be to offer a gratuitous insult to the acuteness of the reader.

XII

An ass meeting a pair of horses, late one evening, said to them:

"It is time all honest horses were in bed. Why are you driving out at this time of day?"

"Ah!" returned they, "if it is so very late, why are you out riding?"

"I never in my life," retorted the ass angrily, "knew a horse to return a direct answer to a civil question."

This tale shows that this ass did not know everything.

[The implication that horses do not answer questions seems to have irritated the worthy fabulist.—TRANSLATOR.]

Ambrose Bierce

XIII

A stone being cast by the plough against a lump of earth, hastened to open the conversation as follows:

"Virtue, which is the opposite of vice, is best fostered by the absence of temptation!"

The lump of earth, being taken somewhat by surprise, was not prepared with an apophthegm, and said nothing.

Since that time it has been customary to call a stupid person a "clod."

XIV

A river seeing a zephyr carrying off an anchor, asked him, "What are you going to do with it?"

"I give it up," replied the zephyr, after mature reflection.

"Blow me if *I* would!" continued the river; "you might just as well not have taken it at all."

"Between you and me," returned the zephyr, "I only picked it up because it is customary for zephyrs to do such things. But if you don't mind I will carry it up to your head and drop it in your mouth."

This fable teaches such a multitude of good things that it would be invidious to mention any.

XV

A peasant sitting on a pile of stones saw an ostrich approaching, and when it had got within range he began pelting it. It is hardly probable that the bird liked this; but it never moved until a large number of boulders had been discharged; then it fell to and ate them.

"It was very good of you, sir," then said the fowl; "pray tell me to what virtue I am indebted for this excellent meal."

"To piety," replied the peasant, who, believing that anything able to devour stones must be a god, was stricken with fear. "I beg you won't think these were merely cold victuals from my table; I had just gathered them fresh, and was intending to have them dressed for my dinner; but I am always hospitable to the deities, and now I suppose I shall have to go without."

"On the contrary, my pious youth," returned the ostrich, "you shall go within."

And the man followed the stones.

The falsehoods of the wicked never amount to much.

XVI

Two thieves went into a farmer's granary and stole a sack of kitchen vegetables; and, one of them slinging it across his shoulders, they began to run away. In a moment all the domestic animals and barn-yard fowls about the place were at their heels, in high clamour, which threatened to bring the farmer down upon them with his dogs.

"You have no idea how the weight of this sack assists me in escaping, by increasing my momentum," said the one who carried the plunder; "suppose *you* take it."

"Ah!" returned the other, who had been zealously pointing out the way to safety, and keeping foremost therein, "it is interesting to find how a common danger makes people confiding. You have a thousand times said I could not be trusted with valuable booty. It is an humiliating confession, but I am myself convinced that if I should assume that sack, and the impetus it confers, you could not depend upon your dividend."

"A common danger," was the reply, "seems to stimulate conviction, as well as confidence."

"Very likely," assented the other, drily; "I am quite too busy to enter into these subtleties. You will find the subject very ably treated in the Zend-Avesta."

But the bastinado taught them more in a minute than they would have gleaned from that excellent work in a fortnight.

If they could only have had the privilege of reading this fable, it would have taught them more than either.

Ambrose Bierce

XVII

While a man was trying with all his might to cross a fence, a bull ran to his assistance, and taking him upon his horns, tossed him over. Seeing the man walking away without making any remark, the bull said:

"You are quite welcome, I am sure. I did no more than my duty."

"I take a different view of it, very naturally," replied the man, "and you may keep your polite acknowledgments of my gratitude until you receive it. I did not require your services."

"You don't mean to say," answered the bull, "that you did not wish to cross that fence!"

"I mean to say," was the rejoinder, "that I wished to cross it by my method, solely to avoid crossing it by yours."

Fabula docet that while the end is everything, the means is something.

XVIII

An hippopotamus meeting an open alligator, said to him:

"My forked friend, you may as well collapse. You are not sufficiently comprehensive to embrace me. I am myself no tyro at smiling, when in the humour."

"I really had no expectation of taking you in," replied the other. "I have a habit of extending my hospitality impartially to all, and about seven feet wide."

"You remind me," said the hippopotamus, "of a certain zebra who was not vicious at all; he merely kicked the breath out of everything that passed behind him, but did not induce things to pass behind him."

"It is quite immaterial what I remind you of," was the reply.

The lesson conveyed by this fable is a very beautiful one.

Ambrose Bierce

XIX

A man was plucking a living goose, when his victim addressed him thus:

"Suppose *you* were a goose; do you think you would relish this sort of thing?"

"Well, suppose I were," answered the man; "do you think *you* would like to pluck me?"

"Indeed I would!" was the emphatic, natural, but injudicious reply.

"Just so," concluded her tormentor; "that's the way *I* feel about the matter."

XX

A traveller perishing of thirst in a desert, debated with his camel whether they should continue their journey, or turn back to an oasis they had passed some days before. The traveller favoured the latter plan.

"I am decidedly opposed to any such waste of time," said the animal; "I don't care for oases myself."

"I should not care for them either," retorted the man, with some temper, "if, like you, I carried a number of assorted water-tanks inside. But as you will not submit to go back, and I shall not consent to go forward, we can only remain where we are."

"But," objected the camel, "that will be certain death to you!"

"Not quite," was the quiet answer, "it involves only the loss of my camel."

So saying, he assassinated the beast, and appropriated his liquid store.

A compromise is not always a settlement satisfactory to both parties.

Ambrose Bierce

XXI

A sheep, making a long journey, found the heat of his fleece very uncomfortable, and seeing a flock of other sheep in a fold, evidently awaiting for some one, leaped over and joined them, in the hope of being shorn. Perceiving the shepherd approaching, and the other sheep huddling into a remote corner of the fold, he shouldered his way forward, and going up to the shepherd, said:

"Did you ever see such a lot of fools? It's lucky I came along to set them an example of docility. Seeing me operated upon, they 'll be glad to offer themselves."

"Perhaps so," replied the shepherd, laying hold of the animal's horns; "but I never kill more than one sheep at a time. Mutton won't keep in hot weather."

The chops tasted excellently well with tomato sauce.

The moral of this fable isn't what you think it is. It is this: The chops of another man's mutton are *always* nice eating.

XXII

Two travellers between Teheran and Bagdad met half-way up the vertical face of a rock, on a path only a cubit in width. As both were in a hurry, and etiquette would allow neither to set his foot upon the other even if dignity had permitted prostration, they maintained for some time a stationary condition. After some reflection, each decided to jump round the other; but as etiquette did not warrant conversation with a stranger, neither made known his intention. The consequence was they met, with considerable emphasis, about four feet from the edge of the path, and went through a flight of soaring eagles, a mile out of their way![A]

[Footnote A: This is infamous! The learned Parsee appears wholly to ignore the distinction between a fable and a simple lie.—TRANSLATOR.]

Ambrose Bierce

XXIII

A stone which had lain for centuries in a hidden place complained to Allah that remaining so long in one position was productive of cramps.

"If thou wouldst be pleased," it said, "to let me take a little exercise now and then, my health would be the better for it."

So it was granted permission to make a short excursion, and at once began rolling out into the open desert. It had not proceeded far before an ostrich, who was pensively eating a keg of nails, left his repast, dashed at the stone, and gobbled it up.

This narration teaches the folly of contentment: if the ostrich had been content with his nails he would never have eaten the stone.

XXIV

A man carrying a sack of corn up a high ladder propped against a wall, had nearly reached the top, when a powerful hog passing that way leant against the bottom to scratch its hide.

"I wish," said the man, speaking down the ladder, "you would make that operation as brief as possible; and when I come down I will reward you by rearing a fresh ladder especially for you."

"This one is quite good enough for a hog," was the reply; "but I am curious to know if you will keep your promise, so I'll just amuse myself until you come down."

And taking the bottom rung in his mouth, he moved off, away from the wall. A moment later he had all the loose corn he could garner, but he never got that other ladder.

MORAL.—An ace and four kings is as good a hand as one can hold in draw-poker.

XXV

A young cock and a hen were speaking of the size of eggs. Said the cock:

"I once laid an egg—"

"Oh, you did!" interrupted the hen, with a derisive cackle. "Pray how did you manage it?"

The cock felt injured in his self-esteem, and, turning his back upon the hen, addressed himself to a brood of young chickens.

"I once laid an egg—"

The chickens chirped incredulously, and passed on. The insulted bird reddened in the wattles with indignation, and strutting up to the patriarch of the entire barn-yard, repeated his assertion. The patriarch nodded gravely, as if the feat were an every-day affair, and the other continued:

"I once laid an egg alongside a water-melon, and compared the two. The vegetable was considerably the larger."

This fable is intended to show the absurdity of hearing all a man has to say.

XXVI

Seeing himself getting beyond his depth, a bathing naturalist called lustily for succour.

"Anything *I* can do for you?" inquired the engaging octopus.

"Happy to serve you, I am sure," said the accommodating leech.

"Command *me*," added the earnest crab.

"Gentlemen of the briny deep," exclaimed the gasping *savant*, "I am compelled to decline your friendly offices, but I tender you my scientific gratitude; and, as a return favour, I beg, with this my last breath, that you will accept the freedom of my aquarium, and make it your home."

This tale proves that scientific gratitude is quite as bad as the natural sort.

Ambrose Bierce

XXVII

Two whales seizing a pike, attempted in turn to swallow him, but without success. They finally determined to try him jointly, each taking hold of an end, and both shutting their eyes for a grand effort, when a shark darted silently between them, biting away the whole body of their prey. Opening their eyes, they gazed upon one another with much satisfaction.

"I had no idea he would go down so easily," said the one.

"Nor I," returned the other; "but how very tasteless a pike is."

The insipidity we observe in most of our acquaintances is largely due to our imperfect knowledge of them.

XXVIII

A wolf went into the cottage of a peasant while the family was absent in the fields, and falling foul of some beef, was quietly enjoying it, when he was observed by a domestic rat, who went directly to her master, informing him of what she had seen.

"I would myself have dispatched the robber," she added, "but feared you might wish to take him alive."

So the man secured a powerful club and went to the door of the house, while the rat looked in at the window. After taking a survey of the situation, the man said:

"I don't think I care to take this fellow alive. Judging from his present performance, I should say his keeping would entail no mean expense. You may go in and slay him if you like; I have quite changed my mind."

"If you really intended taking him prisoner," replied the rat, "the object of that bludgeon is to me a matter of mere conjecture. However, it is easy enough to see you have changed your mind; and it may be barely worth mentioning that I have changed mine."

"The interest you both take in me," said the wolf, without looking up, "touches me deeply. As you have considerately abstained from bothering me with the question of how I am to be disposed of, I will not embarrass your counsels by obtruding a preference. Whatever may be your decision, you may count on my acquiescence; my countenance alone ought to convince you of the meek docility of my character. I never lose my temper, and I never swear; but, by the stomach of the Prophet! if either one of you domestic animals is in sight when I have finished the conquest of these ribs, the question of *my* fate may be postponed for future debate, without detriment to any important interest."

This fable teaches that while you are considering the abatement of a nuisance, it is important to know which nuisance is the more likely to be abated.

XXIX

A snake tried to shed his skin by pulling it off over his head, but, being unable to do so, was advised by a woodman to slip out of it in the usual way.

"But," said the serpent, "this is the way *you* do it!"

"True," exclaimed the woodman, holding out the hem of his tunic; "but you will observe that my skin is brief and open. If you desire one like that, I think I can assist you."

So saying, he chopped off about a cubit of the snake's tail.

Ambrose Bierce

XXX

An oyster who had got a large pebble between the valves of his shell, and was unable to get it out, was lamenting his sad fate, when—the tide being out—a monkey ran to him, and began making an examination.

"You appear," said the monkey, "to have got something else in here, too. I think I'd better remove that first."

With this he inserted his paw, and scooped out the animal's essential part.

"Now," said he, eating the portion he had removed, "I think you will be able to manage the pebble yourself."

To apprehend the lesson of this fable one must have some experience of the law.

XXXI

An old fox and her two cubs were pursued by dogs, when one of the cubs got a thorn in his foot, and could go no farther. Setting the other to watch for the pursuers, the mother proceeded, with much tender solicitude, to extract the thorn. Just as she had done so, the sentinel gave the alarm.

"How near are they?" asked the mother.

"Close by, in the next field," was the answer.

"The deuce they are!" was the hasty rejoinder. "However, I presume they will be content with a single fox."

And shoving the thorn earnestly back into the wounded foot, this excellent parent took to her heels.

This fable proves that humanity does not happen to enjoy a monopoly of paternal affection.

Ambrose Bierce

XXXII

A man crossing the great river of Egypt, heard a voice, which seemed to come from beneath his boat, requesting him to stop. Thinking it must proceed from some river-deity, he laid down his paddle and said:

"Whoever you are that ask me to stop, I beg you will let me go on. I have been asked by a friend to dine with him, and I am late."

"Should your friend pass this way," said the voice, "I will show him the cause of your detention. Meantime you must come to dinner with *me*."

"Willingly," replied the man, devoutly, very well pleased with so extraordinary an honour; "pray show me the way."

"In here," said the crocodile, elevating his distending jaws above the water and beckoning with his tongue—"this way, please."

This fable shows that being asked to dinner is not always the same thing as being asked to dine.

XXXIII

An old monkey, designing to teach his sons the advantage of unity, brought them a number of sticks, and desired them to see how easily they might be broken, one at a time. So each young monkey took a stick and broke it.

"Now," said the father, "I will teach you a lesson."

And he began to gather the sticks into a bundle. But the young monkeys, thinking he was about to beat them, set upon him, all together, and disabled him.

"There!" said the aged sufferer, "behold the advantage of unity! If you had assailed me one at a time, I would have killed every mother's son of you!"

Moral lessons are like the merchant's goods: they are conveyed in various ways.

Ambrose Bierce

XXXIV

A wild horse meeting a domestic one, taunted him with his condition of servitude. The tamed animal claimed that he was as free as the wind.

"If that is so," said the other, "pray tell me the office of that bit in your mouth."

"That," was the answer, "is iron, one of the best tonics in the *materia medica.*"

"But what," said the other, "is the meaning of the rein attached to it?"

"Keeps it from falling out of my mouth when I am too indolent to hold it," was the reply.

"How about the saddle?"

"Fool!" was the angry retort; "its purpose is to spare me fatigue: when I am tired, I get on and ride."

XXXV

Some doves went to a hawk, and asked him to protect them from a kite.

"That I will," was the cheerful reply; "and when I am admitted into the dovecote, I shall kill more of you in a day than the kite did in a century. But of course you know this; you expect to be treated in the regular way."

So he entered the dovecote, and began preparations for a general slaughter. But the doves all set upon him and made exceedingly short work of him. With his last breath he asked them why, being so formidable, they had not killed the kite. They replied that they had never seen any kite.

Ambrose Bierce

XXXVI

A defeated warrior snatched up his aged father, and, slinging him across his shoulders, plunged into the wilderness, followed by the weary remnant of his beaten army. The old gentleman liked it.

"See!" said he, triumphantly, to the flying legion; "did you ever hear of so dutiful and accommodating a son? And he's as easy unde the saddle as an old family horse!"

"I rather think," replied the broken and disordered battalion, with a grin, "that Mr. AEneas once did something of this kind. But *his* father had thoughtfully taken an armful of lares and penates; and the accommodating nature of *his* son was, therefore, more conspicuous. If I might venture to suggest that you take up my shield and scimitar—"

"Thank you," said the aged party, "I could not think of disarming the military: but if you would just hand me up one of the heaviest of those dead branches, I think the merits of my son would be rendered sufficiently apparent."

The routed column passed him up the one shown in the immediate foreground of our sketch, and it was quite enough for both steed and rider.

Fabula ostendit that History repeats itself, with variations.

XXXVII

A pig who had engaged a cray-fish to pilot him along the beach in search of mussels, was surprised to see his guide start off backwards.

"Your excessive politeness quite overcomes me," said the porker, "but don't you think it rather ill bestowed upon a pig? Pray don't hesitate to turn your back upon me."

"Sir," replied the cray-fish, "permit me to continue as I am. We now stand to each other in the proper relation of *employe* to employer. The former is excessively obsequious, and the latter is, in the eyes of the former, a hog."

Ambrose Bierce

XXXVIII

The king of tortoises desiring to pay a visit of ceremony to a neighbouring monarch, feared that in his absence his idle subjects might get up a revolution, and that whoever might be left at the head of the State would usurp the throne. So calling his subjects about him, he addressed them thus:

"I am about to leave our beloved country for a long period, and desire to leave the sceptre in the hands of him who is most truly a tortoise. I decree that you shall set out from yonder distant tree, and pass round it. Whoever shall get back last shall be appointed Regent."

So the population set out for the goal, and the king for his destination. Before the race was decided, his Majesty had made the journey and returned. But he found the throne occupied by a subject, who at once secured by violence what he had won by guile.

Certain usurpers are too conscientious to retain kingly power unless the rightful monarch be dead; and these are the most dangerous sort.

XXXIX

A spaniel at the point of death requested a mastiff friend to eat him.

"It would soothe my last moments," said he, "to know that when I am no longer of any importance to myself I may still be useful to you."

"Much obliged, I am sure," replied his friend; "I think you mean well, but you should know that my appetite is not so depraved as to relish dog."

Perhaps it is for a similar reason we abstain from cannibalism.

Ambrose Bierce

XL

A cloud was passing across the face of the sun, when the latter expostulated with him.

"Why," said the sun, "when you have so much space to float in, should you be casting your cold shadow upon me?"

After a moment's reflection, the cloud made answer thus:

"I certainly had no intention of giving offence by my presence, and as for my shadow, don't you think you have made a trifling mistake?—not a gigantic or absurd mistake, but merely one that would disgrace an idiot."

At this the great luminary was furious, and fell so hotly upon him that in a few minutes there was nothing of him left.

It is very foolish to bandy words with a cloud if you happen to be the sun.

XLI

A rabbit travelling leisurely along the highway was seen, at some distance, by a duck, who had just come out of the water.

"Well, I declare!" said she, "if I could not walk without limping in that ridiculous way, I'd stay at home. Why, he's a spectacle!"

"Did you ever see such an ungainly beast as that duck!" said the rabbit to himself. "If I waddled like that I should go out only at night."

MORAL, BY A KANGAROO.—People who are ungraceful of gait are always intolerant of mind.

XLII

A fox who dwelt in the upper chamber of an abandoned watch-tower, where he practised all manner of magic, had by means of his art subjected all other animals to his will. One day he assembled a great multitude of them below his window, and commanded that each should appear in his presence, and all who could not teach him some important truth should be thrown off the walls and dashed to pieces. Upon hearing this they were all stricken with grief, and began to lament their hard fate most piteously.

"How," said they, "shall we, who are unskilled in magic, unread in philosophy, and untaught in the secrets of the stars—who have neither wit, eloquence, nor song—how shall we essay to teach wisdom to the wise?"

Nevertheless, they were compelled to make the attempt. After many had failed and been dispatched, another fox arrived on the ground, and learning the condition of affairs, scampered slyly up the steps, and whispered something in the ear of the cat, who was about entering the tower. So the latter stuck her head in at the door, and shrieked:

"Pullets with a southern exposure ripen earliest, and have yellow legs."

At this the magician was so delighted that he dissolved the spell and let them all go free.

XLIII

One evening a jackass, passing between a village and a hill, looked over the latter and saw the faint light of the rising moon.

"Ho-ho, Master Redface!" said he, "so you are climbing up the other side to point out my long ears to the villagers, are you? I'll just meet you at the top, and set my heels into your insolent old lantern."

So he scrambled painfully up to the crest, and stood outlined against the broad disc of the unconscious luminary, more conspicuously a jackass than ever before.

Ambrose Bierce

XLIV

A bear wishing to rob a beehive, laid himself down in front of it, and overturned it with his paw.

"Now," said he, "I will lie perfectly still and let the bees sting me until they are exhausted and powerless; their honey may then be obtained without opposition."

And it was so obtained, but by a fresh bear, the other being dead.

This narrative exhibits one aspect of the "Fabian policy."

XLV

A cat seeing a mouse with a piece of cheese, said:

"I would not eat that, if I were you, for I think it is poisoned. However, if you will allow me to examine it, I will tell you certainly whether it is or not."

While the mouse was thinking what it was best to do, the cat had fully made up her mind, and was kind enough to examine both the cheese and the mouse in a manner highly satisfactory to herself, but the mouse has never returned to give *his* opinion.

Ambrose Bierce

XLVI

An improvident man, who had quarrelled with his wife concerning household expenses, took her and the children out on the
lawn, intending to make an example of her. Putting himself in
an attitude of aggression, and turning to his offspring, he said:

"You will observe, my darlings, that domestic offences are
always punished with a loss of blood. Make a note of this and
be wise."

He had no sooner spoken than a starving mosquito settled
upon his nose, and began to assist in enforcing the lesson.

"My officious friend," said the man, "when I require illustra-
tions from the fowls of the air, you may command my
patronage. The deep interest you take in my affairs is, at
present, a trifle annoying."

"I do not find it so," the mosquito would have replied had he
been at leisure, "and am convinced that our respective points
of view are so widely dissimilar as not to afford the faintest
hope of reconciling our opinions upon collateral points. Let us
be thankful that upon the main question of bloodletting we
perfectly agree."

When the bird had concluded, the man's convictions were
quite unaltered, but he was too weak to resume the discussion;
and, although blood is thicker than water, the children were
constrained to confess that the stranger had the best of it.

This fable teaches.

XLVII

"I hate snakes who bestow their caresses with interested partiality or fastidious discrimination," boasted a boa constrictor. "*My* affection is unbounded; it embraces all animated nature. I am the universal shepherd; I gather all manner of living things into my folds. Entertainment here for man and beast!"

"I should be glad of one of your caresses," said a porcupine, meekly; "it has been some time since I got a loving embrace."

So saying, he nestled snugly and confidingly against the large-hearted serpent—who fled.

A comprehensive philanthropy may be devoid of prejudices, but it has its preferences all the same.

XLVIII

During a distressing famine in China a starving man met a fat pig, who, seeing no chance of escape, walked confidently up to the superior animal, and said:

"Awful famine! isn't it?"

"Quite dreadful!" replied the man, eyeing him with an evident purpose: "almost impossible to obtain meat."

"Plenty of meat, such as it is, but no corn. Do you know, I have been compelled to eat so many of your people, I don't believe there is an ounce of pork in my composition."

"And I so many that I have lost all taste for pork."

"Terrible thing this cannibalism!"

"Depends upon which character you try it in; it is terrible to be eaten."

"You are very brutal!"

"You are very fat."

"You look as if you would take my life."

"You look as if you would sustain mine."

"Let us 'pull sticks,'" said the now desperate animal, "to see which of us shall die."

"Good!" assented the man: "I'll pull this one."

So saying, he drew a hedge-stake from the ground, and stained it with the brain of that unhappy porker.

MORAL.—An empty stomach has no ears.

Ambrose Bierce

XLIX

A snake, a mile long, having drawn himself over a roc's egg, complained that in its present form he could get no benefit from it, and modestly desired the roc to aid him in some way.

"Certainly," assented the bird, "I think we can arrange it."

Saying which, she snatched up one of the smaller Persian provinces, and poising herself a few leagues above the suffering reptile, let it drop upon him to smash the egg.

This fable exhibits the folly of asking for aid without specifying the kind and amount of aid you require.

L

An ox meeting a man on the highway, asked him for a pinch of snuff, whereupon the man fled back along the road in extreme terror.

"*Don't* be alarmed," said a horse whom he met; "the ox won't bite you."

The man gave one stare and dashed across the meadows.

"Well," said a sheep, "I wouldn't be afraid of a horse; *he* won't kick."

The man shot like a comet into the forest.

"Look where you're going there, or I'll thrash the life out of you!" screamed a bird into whose nest he had blundered.

Frantic with fear, the man leapt into the sea.

"By Jove! how you frightened me," said a small shark.

The man was dejected, and felt a sense of injury. He seated himself moodily on the bottom, braced up his chin with his knees, and thought for an hour. Then he beckoned to the fish who had made the last remark.

"See here, I say," said he, "I wish you would just tell me what in thunder this all means."

"Ever read any fables?" asked the shark.

"No—yes—well, the catechism, the marriage service, and—"

"Oh, bother!" said the fish, playfully, smiling clean back to the pectoral fins; "get out of this and bolt your AEsop!"

The man did get out and bolted.

[This fable teaches that its worthy author was drunk as a loon.—TRANSLATOR.]

LI

A lion pursued by some villagers was asked by a fox why he did not escape on horseback.

"There is a fine strong steed just beyond this rock," said the fox. "All you have to do is to get on his back and stay there."

So the lion went up to the charger and asked him to give him a lift.

"Certainly," said the horse, "with great pleasure."

And setting one of his heels into the animal's stomach, he lifted him. about seven feet from the ground.

"Confound you!" roared the beast as he fell back.

"So did you," quietly remarked the steed.

Ambrose Bierce

LII

A Mahout who had dismounted from his elephant, and was quietly standing on his head in the middle of the highway, was asked by the animal why he did not revert and move on.

"You are making a spectacle of yourself," said the beast.

"If I choose to stand upside down," replied the man, "I am very well aware that I incur the displeasure of those who adhere with slavish tenacity to the prejudices and traditions of society; but it seems to me that rebuke would come with a more consistent grace from one who does not wear a tail upon his nose."

This fable teaches that four straight lines may enclose a circle, but there will be corners to let.

LIII

A dog meeting a strange cat, took her by the top of the back, and shook her for a considerable period with some earnestness. Then depositing her in a ditch, he remarked with gravity:

"There, my feline friend! I think that will teach you a wholesome lesson; and as punishment is intended to be reformatory, you ought to be grateful to me for deigning to administer it."

"I don't think of questioning your right to worry me," said the cat, getting her breath, "but I should like to know where you got your licence to preach at me. Also, if not inconsistent with the dignity of the court, I should wish to be informed of the nature of my offence; in order that I may the more clearly apprehend the character of the lesson imparted by its punishment."

"Since you are so curious," replied the dog, "I worry you because you are too feeble to worry me."

"In other words," rejoined the cat, getting herself together as well as she could, "you bite me for that to which you owe your existence."

The reply of the dog was lost in the illimitable field of ether, whither he was just then projected by the kick of a passing horse. The moral of this fable cannot be given until he shall get down, and close the conversation with the regular apophthegm.

Ambrose Bierce

LIV

People who wear tight hats will do well to lay this fable well to heart, and ponder upon the deep significance of its moral:

In passing over a river, upon a high bridge, a cow discovered a broad loose plank in the flooring, sustained in place by a beam beneath the centre.

"Now," said she, "I will stand at this end of the trap, and when yonder sheep steps upon the opposite extreme there will be an upward tendency in wool."

So when the meditative mutton advanced unwarily upon the treacherous device, the cow sprang bodily upon the other end, and there was a fall in beef.

LV

Two snakes were debating about the proper method of attacking prey.

"The best way," said one, "is to slide cautiously up, endwise, and seize it thus"—illustrating his method by laying hold of the other's tail.

"Not at all," was the reply; "a better plan is to approach by a circular side-sweep, thus"—turning upon his opponent and taking in *his* tail.

Although there was no disagreement as to the manner of disposing of what was once seized, each began to practise his system upon the other, and continued until both were swallowed.

The work begun by contention is frequently completed by habit.

A man staggering wearily through the streets of Persepolis, under a heavy burden, said to himself:

"I wish I knew what this thing is I have on my back; then I could make some sort of conjecture as to what I design doing with it."

"Suppose," said the burden, "I were a man in a sack; what disposition would you make of me?"

"The regular thing," replied the man, "would be to take you over to Constantinople, and pitch you into the Bosphorus; but I should probably content myself with laying you down and jumping on you, as being more agreeable to my feelings, and quite as efficacious."

"But suppose," continued the burden, "I were a shoulder of beef—which I quite as much resemble—belonging to some poor family?"

"In that case," replied the man, promptly, "I should carry you to my larder, my good fellow."

"But if I were a sack of gold, do you think you would find me very onerous?" said the burden.

"A great deal would depend," was the answer, "upon whom you happened to belong to; but I may say, generally, that gold upon the shoulders is wonderfully light, considering the weight of it."

"Behold," said the burden, "the folly of mankind: they cannot perceive that the *quality* of the burdens of life is a matter of no importance. The question of pounds and ounces is the only consideration of any real weight."

LVII

A ghost meeting a genie, one wintry night, said to him:

"Extremely harassing weather, friend. Wish I had some teeth to chatter!"

"You do not need them," said the other; "you can always chatter those of other people, by merely showing yourself. For my part, I should be content with some light employment: would erect a cheap palace, transport a light-weight princess, threaten a small cripple—or jobs of that kind. What are the prospects of the fool crop?"

"For the next few thousand years, very good. There is a sort of thing called Literature coming in shortly, and it will make our fortune. But it will be very bad for History. Curse this phantom apparel! The more I gather it about me the colder I get."

"When Literature has made our fortune," sneered the genie, "I presume you will purchase material clothing."

"And you," retorted the ghost, "will be able to advertise for permanent employment at a fixed salary."

This fable shows the difference between the super natural and the natural "super": the one appears in the narrative, the other does not.

LVIII

"Permit me to help you on in the world, sir," said a boy to a travelling tortoise, placing a glowing coal upon the animal's back.

"Thank you," replied the unconscious beast; "I alone am responsible for the time of my arrival, and I alone will determine the degree of celerity required. The gait I am going will enable me to keep all my present appointments."

A genial warmth began about this time to pervade his upper crust, and a moment after he was dashing away at a pace comparatively tremendous.

"How about those engagements?" sneered the grinning urchin.

"I've recollected another one," was the hasty reply.

LIX

Having fastened his gaze upon a sparrow, a rattlesnake sprung open his spanning jaws, and invited her to enter.

"I should be most happy," said the bird, not daring to betray her helpless condition, but anxious by any subterfuge to get the serpent to remove his fascinating regard, "but I am lost in contemplation of yonder green sunset, from which I am unable to look away for more than a minute. I shall turn to it presently."

"Do, by all means," said the serpent, with a touch of irony in his voice. "There is nothing so improving as a good, square, green sunset."

"Did you happen to observe that man standing behind you with a club?" continued the sparrow. "Handsome fellow! Fifteen cubits high, with seven heads, and very singularly attired; quite a spectacle in his way."

"I don't seem to care much for men," said the snake. "Every way inferior to serpents—except in malice."

"But he is accompanied by a *really interesting* child," persisted the bird, desperately.

The rattlesnake reflected deeply. He soliloquized as follows:

"There is a mere chance—say about one chance to ten thousand million—that this songster is speaking the truth. One chance in ten thousand million of seeing a really interesting child is worth the sacrifice demanded; I'll make it."

So saying, he removed his glittering eyes from the bird (who immediately took wing) and looked behind him. It is needless to say there was no really interesting child there—nor anywhere else.

MORAL.—Mendacity (so called from the inventors) is a very poor sort of dacity; but it will serve your purpose if you draw it sufficiently strong.

LX

A man who was very much annoyed by the incursions of a lean ass belonging to his neighbour, resolved to compass the destruction of the invader.

"Now," said he, "if this animal shall choose to starve himself to death in the midst of plenty, the law will not hold *me* guilty of his blood. I have read of a trick which I think will 'fix' him."

So he took two bales of his best hay, and placed them in a distant field, about forty cubits apart. By means of a little salt he then enticed the ass in, and coaxed him between the bundles.

"There, fiend!" said he, with a diabolic grin, as he walked away delighted with the success of his stratagem, "now hesitate which bundle of hay to attack first, until you starve— monster!"

Some weeks afterwards he returned with a wagon to convey back the bundles of hay. There wasn't any hay, but the wagon was useful for returning to his owner that unfortunate ass— who was too fat to walk.

This ought to show any one the folly of relying upon the teaching of obscure and inferior authors.[A]

[Footnote A: It is to be wished our author had not laid himself open to the imputation of having perverted, if not actually invented, some of his facts, for the unworthy purpose of bringing a deserving rival into disfavour.—TRANSLATOR.]

Ambrose Bierce

LXI

One day the king of the wrens held his court for the trial of a bear, who was at large upon his own recognizance. Being summoned to appear, the animal came with great humility into the royal presence.

"What have you to say, sir," demanded the king, "in defence of your inexcusable conduct in pillaging the nests of our loyal subjects wherever you can find them?"

"May it please your Majesty," replied the prisoner, with a reverential gesture, repeated at intervals, and each time at a less distance from the royal person, "I will not wound your Majesty's sensibilities by pleading a love of eggs; I will humbly confess my course of crime, warn your Majesty of its probable continuance, and beg your Majesty's gracious permission to inquire—What is your Majesty going to do about it?"

The king and his ministers were very much struck with this respectful speech, with the ingenuity of the final inquiry, and with the bear's paw. It was the paw, however, which made the most lasting impression.

Always give ear to the flattery of your powerful inferiors: it will cheer you in your decline.

LXII

A philosopher looking up from the pages of the Zend-Avesta, upon which he had been centring his soul, beheld a pig violently assailing a cauldron of cold slops.

"Heaven bless us!" said the sage; "for unalloyed delight give me a good honest article of Sensuality. So soon as my 'Essay upon the Correlation of Mind-forces' shall have brought me fame and fortune, I hope to abjure the higher faculties, devoting the remainder of my life to the cultivation of the propensities."

"Allah be praised!" soliloquized the pig, "there is nothing so godlike as Intellect, and nothing so ecstatic as intellectual pursuits. I must hasten to perform this gross material function, that I may retire to my wallow and resign my soul to philosophical meditation."

This tale has one moral if you are a philosopher, and another if you are a pig.

Ambrose Bierce

"Awful dark—isn't it?" said an owl, one night, looking in upon the roosting hens in a poultry-house; "don't see how I am to find my way back to my hollow tree."

"There is no necessity," replied the cock; "you can roost there, alongside the door, and go home in the morning."

"Thanks!" said the owl, chuckling at the fool's simplicity; and, having plenty of time to indulge his facetious humour, he gravely installed himself upon the perch indicated, and shutting his eyes, counterfeited a profound slumber. He was aroused soon after by a sharp constriction of the throat.

"I omitted to tell you," said the cock, "that the seat you happen by the merest chance to occupy is a contested one, and has been fruitful of hens to this vexatious weasel. I don't know *how* often I have been partially widowed by the sneaking villain."

For obvious reasons there was no audible reply.

This narrative is intended to teach the folly—the worse than sin!—of trumping your partner's ace.

LXIV

A fat cow who saw herself detected by an approaching horse while perpetrating stiff and ungainly gambols in the spring sunshine, suddenly assumed a severe gravity of gait, and a sedate solemnity of expression that would have been creditable to a Brahmin.

"Fine morning!" said the horse, who, fired by her example, was curvetting lithely and tossing his head.

"That rather uninteresting fact," replied the cow, attending strictly to her business as a ruminant, "does not impress me as justifying your execution of all manner of unseemly contortions, as a preliminary to accosting an entire stranger."

"Well, n—no," stammered the horse; "I—I suppose not. Fact is I—I—no offence, I hope."

And the unhappy charger walked soberly away, dazed by the preternatural effrontery of that placid cow.

When overcome by the dignity of any one you chance to meet, try to have this fable about you.

LXV

"What have you there on your back?" said a zebra, jeeringly, to a "ship of the desert" in ballast.

"Only a bale of gridirons," was the meek reply.

"And what, pray, may you design doing with them?" was the incredulous rejoinder.

"What am I to do with gridirons?" repeated the camel, contemptuously. "Nice question for *you*, who have evidently just come off one!"

People who wish to throw stones should not live in glass houses; but there ought to be a few in their vicinity.

LXVI

A cat, waking out of a sound sleep, saw a mouse sitting just out of reach, observing her. Perceiving that at the slightest movement of hers the mouse would recollect an engagement, she put on a look of extreme amiability, and said:

"Oh! it's you, is it? Do you know, I thought at first you were a frightful great rat; and I am *so* afraid of rats! I feel so much relieved—you don't know! Of course you have heard that I am a great friend to the dear little mice?"

"Yes," was the answer, "I have heard that you love us indifferently well, and my mission here was to bless you while you slept. But as you will wish to go and get your breakfast, I won't bore you. Fine morning—isn't it? *Au revoir!*"

This fable teaches that it is usually safe to avoid one who pretends to be a friend without having any reason to be. It wasn't safe in this instance, however; for the cat went after that departing rodent, and got away with him.

LXVII

A man pursued by a lion, was about stepping into a place of safety, when he bethought him of the power of the human eye; and, turning about, he fixed upon his pursuer a steady look of stern reproof. The raging beast immediately moderated his rate per hour, and finally came to a dead halt, within a yard of the man's nose. After making a leisurely survey of him, he extended his neck and bit off a small section of his victim's thigh.

"Beard of Arimanes!" roared the man; "have you no respect for the Human Eye?"

"I hold the human eye in profound esteem," replied the lion, "and I confess its power. It assists digestion if taken just before a meal. But I don't understand why you should have two and I none."

With that he raised his foot, unsheathed his claws, and transferred one of the gentleman's visual organs to his own mouth.

"Now," continued he, "during the brief remainder of a squandered existence, your lion-quelling power, being more highly concentrated, will be the more easily managed."

He then devoured the remnant of his victim, including the other eye.

LXVIII

An ant laden with a grain of corn, which he had acquired with infinite toil, was breasting a current of his fellows, each of whom, as is their etiquette, insisted upon stopping him, feeling him all over, and shaking hands. It occurred to him that an excess of ceremony is an abuse of courtesy. So he laid down his burden, sat upon it, folded all his legs tight to his body, and smiled a smile of great grimness.

"Hullo! what's the matter with *you*?" exclaimed the first insect whose overtures were declined.

"Sick of the hollow conventionalities of a rotten civilization," was the rasping reply. "Relapsed into the honest simplicity of primitive observances. Go to grass!"

"Ah! then we must trouble you for that corn. In a condition of primitive simplicity there are no rights of property, you know. These are 'hollow conventionalities.'"

A light dawned upon the intellect of that pismire. He shook the reefs out of his legs; he scratched the reverse of his ear; he grappled that cereal, and trotted away like a giant refreshed. It was observed that he submitted with a wealth of patience to manipulation by his friends and neighbours, and went some distance out of his way to shake hands with strangers on competing lines of traffic.

LXIX

A snake who had lain torpid all winter in his hole took advantage of the first warm day to limber up for the spring campaign. Having tied himself into an intricate knot, he was so overcome by the warmth of his own body that he fell asleep, and did not wake until nightfall. In the darkness he was unable to find his head or his tail, and so could not disentangle and slide into his hole. Per consequence, he froze to death.

Many a subtle philosopher has failed to solve himself, owing to his inability to discern his beginning and his end.

A dog finding a joint of mutton, apparently guarded by a negligent raven, stretched himself before it with an air of intense satisfaction.

"Ah!" said he, alternately smiling and stopping up the smiles with meat, "this is an instrument of salvation to my stomach— an instrument upon which I love to perform."

"I beg your pardon!" said the bird; "it was placed there specially for me, by one whose right to so convey it is beyond question, he having legally acquired it by chopping it off the original owner."

"I detect no flaw in your abstract of title," replied the dog; "all seems quite regular; but I must not provoke a breach of the peace by lightly relinquishing what I might feel it my duty to resume by violence. I must have time to consider; and in the meantime I will dine."

Thereupon he leisurely consumed the property in dispute, shut his eyes, yawned, turned upon his back, thrust out his legs divergently, and died.

For the meat had been carefully poisoned—a fact of which the raven was guiltily conscious.

There are several things mightier than brute force, and arsenic[A] is one of them.

[Footnote A: In the original, "*pizen;*" which might, perhaps, with equal propriety have been rendered by "caper sauce." —TRANSLATOR.]

Ambrose Bierce

LXXI

The King of Persia had a favourite hawk. One day his Majesty was hunting, and had become separated from his attendants. Feeling thirsty, he sought a stream of water trickling from a rock; took a cup, and pouring some liquor into it from his pocket-flask, filled it up with water, and raised it to his lips. The hawk, who had been all this time hovering about, swooped down, screaming "No, you don't!" and upset the cup with his wing.

"I know what is the matter," said the King: "there is a dead serpent in the fountain above, and this faithful bird has saved my life by not permitting me to drink the juice. I must reward him in the regular way."

So he called a page, who had thoughtfully presented himself, and gave directions to have the Remorse Apartments of the palace put in order, and for the court tailor to prepare an evening suit of sackcloth-and-ashes. Then summoning the hawk, he seized and dashed him to the ground, killing him very dead. Rejoining his retinue, he dispatched an officer to remove the body of the serpent from the fountain, lest somebody else should get poisoned. There wasn't any serpent—the water was remarkable for its wholesome purity!

Then the King, cheated of his remorse, was sorry he had slain the bird; he said it was a needless waste of power to kill a bird who merely deserved killing. It never occurred to the King that the hawk's touching solicitude was with reference to the contents of the royal flask.

Fabula ostendit that a "twice-told tale" needs not necessarily be "tedious"; a reasonable degree of interest may be obtained by intelligently varying the details.

LXXII

A herd of cows, blown off the summit of the Himalayas, were sailing some miles above the valleys, when one said to another:

"Got anything to say about this?"

"Not much," was the answer. "It's airy."

"I wasn't thinking of that," continued the first; "I am troubled about our course. If we could leave the Pleiades a little more to the right, striking a middle course between Booetes and the ecliptic, we should find it all plain sailing as far as the solstitial colure. But once we get into the Zodiac upon our present bearing, we are certain to meet with shipwreck before reaching our aphelion."

They escaped this melancholy fate, however, for some Chaldean shepherds, seeing a nebulous cloud drifting athwart the heavens, and obscuring a favourite planet they had just invented, brought out their most powerful telescopes and resolved it into independent cows—whom they proceeded to slaughter in detail with the instruments of smaller calibre. There have been occasional "meat showers" ever since. These are probably nothing more than—

[Our author can be depended upon in matters of fact; his scientific theories are not worth printing.—TRANSLATOR.]

LXXIII

A bear, who had worn himself out walking from one end of his cage to the other, addressed his keeper thus:

"I say, friend, if you don't procure me a shorter cage I shall have to give up zoology; it is about the most wearing pursuit I ever engaged in. I favour the advancement of science, but the mechanical part of it is a trifle severe, and ought to be done by contract."

"You are quite right, my hearty," said the keeper, "it *is* severe; and there have been several excellent plans proposed to lighten the drudgery. Pending the adoption of some of them, you would find a partial relief in lying down and keeping quiet."

"It won't do—it won't do!" replied the bear, with a mournful shake of the head, "it's not the orthodox thing. Inaction may do for professors, collectors, and others connected with the ornamental part of the noble science; but for *us*, we must keep moving, or zoology would soon revert to the crude guesses and mistaken theories of the azoic period. And yet," continued the beast, after the keeper had gone, "there is something novel and ingenious in what the underling suggests. I must remember that; and when I have leisure, give it a trial."

It was noted next day that the noble science had lost an active apostle, and gained a passive disciple.

LXXIV

A hen who had hatched out a quantity of ducklings, was somewhat surprised one day to see them take to the water, and sail away out of her jurisdiction. The more she thought of this the more unreasonable such conduct appeared, and the more indignant she became. She resolved that it must cease forthwith. So she soon afterward convened her brood, and conducted them to the margin of a hot pool, having a business connection with the boiling spring of Doo-sno-swair. They straightway launched themselves for a cruise—returning immediately to the land, as if they had forgotten their ship's papers.

When Callow Youth exhibits an eccentric tendency, give it him hot.

LXXV

"Did it ever occur to you that this manner of thing is extremely unpleasant?" asked a writhing worm of the angler who had impaled him upon a hook. "Such treatment by those who boast themselves our brothers is, possibly, fraternal—but it hurts."

"I confess," replied the idler, "that our usages with regard to vermin and reptiles might be so amended as to be more temperately diabolical; but please to remember that the gentle agonies with which we afflict *you* are wholesome and exhilarating compared with the ills we ladle out to one another. During the reign of His Pellucid Refulgence, Khatchoo Khan," he continued, absently dropping his wriggling auditor into the brook, "no less than three hundred thousand Persian subjects were put to death, in a pleasing variety of ingenious ways, for their religious beliefs."

"What that has to do with your treatment of *us*" interrupted a fish, who, having bitten at the worm just then, was drawn into the conversation, "I am quite unable to see."

"That," said the angler, disengaging him, "is because you have the hook through your eyeball, my edible friend."

Many a truth is spoken in jest; but at least ten times as many falsehoods are uttered in dead earnest.

LXXVI

A wild cat was listening with rapt approval to the melody of distant hounds tracking a remote fox.

"Excellent! *bravo!*" she exclaimed at intervals. "I could sit and listen all day to the like of that. I am passionately fond of music. *Ong-core!*"

Presently the tuneful sounds drew near, whereupon she began to fidget; ending by shinning up a tree, just as the dogs burst into view below her, and stifled their songs upon the body of their victim before her eyes—which protruded.

"There is an indefinable charm," said she—"a subtle and tender spell—a mystery—a conundrum, as it were—in the sounds of an unseen orchestra. This is quite lost when the performers are visible to the audience. Distant music (if any) for your obedient servant!"

Ambrose Bierce

LXXVII

Having been taught to turn his scraps of bad Persian into choice Latin, a parrot was puffed up with conceit.

"Observe," said he, "the superiority I may boast by virtue of my classical education: I can chatter flat nonsense in the language of Cicero."

"I would advise you," said his master, quietly, "to let it be of a different character from that chattered by some of Mr. Cicero's most admired compatriots, if you value the priviledge of hanging at that public window. 'Commit no mythology,' please."

The exquisite fancies of a remote age may not be imitated in this; not, perhaps, from a lack of talent, so much as from a fear of arrest.

LXXVIII

A rat, finding a file, smelt it all over, bit it gently, and observed that, as it did not seem to be rich enough to produce dyspepsia, he would venture to make a meal of it. So he gnawed it into *smithareens*[A] without the slightest injury to his teeth. With his morals the case was somewhat different. For the file was a file of newspapers, and his system became so saturated with the "spirit of the Press" that he went off and called his aged father a "lingering contemporary;" advised the correction of brief tails by amputation; lauded the skill of a quack rodentist for money; and, upon what would otherwise have been his death-bed, essayed a lie of such phenomenal magnitude that it stuck in his throat, and prevented him breathing his last. All this crime, and misery, and other nonsense, because he was too lazy to worry about and find a file of nutritious fables.

This tale shows the folly of eating everything you happen to fancy. Consider, moreover, the danger of such a course to your neighbour's wife.

[Footnote A: I confess my inability to translate this word: it may mean "flinders."—TRANSLATOR.]

LXXIX

"I should like to climb up you, if you don't mind," cried an ivy to a young oak.

"Oh, certainly; come along," was the cheerful assent.

So she started up, and finding she could grow faster than he, she wound round and round him until she had passed up all the line she had. The oak, however, continued to grow, and as she could not disengage her coils, she was just lifted out by the root. So that ends the oak-and-ivy business, and removes a powerful temptation from the path of the young writer.

LXXX

A merchant of Cairo gave a grand feast. In the midst of the revelry, the great doors of the dining-hall were pushed open from the outside, and the guests were surprised and grieved by the advent of a crocodile of a tun's girth, and as long as the moral law.

"Thought I 'd look in," said he, simply, but not without a certain grave dignity.

"But," cried the host, from the top of the table, "I did not invite any saurians."

"No—I know yer didn't; it's the old thing, it is: never no wacancies for saurians—saurians should orter keep theirselves *to* theirselves—no saurians need apply. I got it all by 'eart, I tell yer. But don't give yerself no distress; I didn't come to beg; thank 'eaven I ain't drove to that yet—leastwise I ain't done it. But I thought as 'ow yer'd need a dish to throw slops and broken wittles in it; which I fetched along this 'ere."

And the willing creature lifted off the cover by erecting the upper half of his head till the snout of him smote the ceiling.

Open servitude is better than covert begging.

Ambrose Bierce

LXXXI

A gander being annoyed by the assiduous attendance of his ugly reflection in the water, determined that he would prosecute future voyages in a less susceptible element. So he essayed a sail upon the placid bosom of a clay-bank. This kind of navigation did not meet his expectations, however, and he returned with dogged despair to his pond, resolved to make a final cruise and go out of commission. He was delighted to find that the clay adhering to his hull so defiled the water that it gave back no image of him. After that, whenever he left port, he was careful to be well clayed along the water-line.

The lesson of this is that if all geese are alike, we can banish unpleasant reflections by befouling ourselves. This is worth knowing.

LXXXII

The belly and the members of the human body were in a riot. (This is not the riot recorded by an inferior writer, but a more notable and authentic one.) After exhausting the well-known arguments, they had recourse to the appropriate threat, when the man to whom they belonged thought it time for *him* to be heard, in his capacity as a unit.

"Deuce take you!" he roared. "Things have come to a pretty pass if a fellow cannot walk out of a fine morning without alarming the town by a disgraceful squabble between his component parts! I am reasonably impartial, I hope, but man's devotion is due to his deity: I espouse the cause of my belly."

Hearing this, the members were thrown into so extraordinary confusion that the man was arrested for a windmill.

As a rule, don't "take sides." Sides of bacon, however, may be temperately acquired.

LXXXIII

A man dropping from a balloon struck against a soaring eagle.

"I beg your pardon," said he, continuing his descent; "I never *could* keep off eagles when in my descending node."

"It is agreeable to meet so pleasing a gentleman, even without previous appointment," said the bird, looking admiringly down upon the lessening aeronaut; "he is the very pink of politeness. How extremely nice his liver must be. I will follow him down and arrange his simple obsequies."

This fable is narrated for its intrinsic worth.

LXXXIV

To escape from a peasant who had come suddenly upon him, an opossum adopted his favourite expedient of counterfeiting death.

"I suppose," said the peasant, "that ninety-nine men in a hundred would go away and leave this poor creature's body to the beasts of prey." [It is notorious that man is the only living thing that will eat the animal.] "But *I* will give him good burial."

So he dug a hole, and was about tumbling him into it, when a solemn voice appeared to emanate from the corpse: "Let the dead bury their dead!"

"Whatever spirit hath wrought this miracle," cried the peasant, dropping upon his knees, "let him but add the trifling explanation of *how* the dead can perform this or any similar rite, and I am obedience itself. Otherwise, in goes Mr. 'Possum by these hands."

"Ah!" meditated the unhappy beast, "I have performed one miracle, but I can't keep it up all day, you know. The explanation demanded is a trifle too heavy for even the ponderous ingenuity of a marsupial."

And he permitted himself to be sodded over.

If the reader knows what lesson is conveyed by this narrative, he knows—just what the writer knows.

Ambrose Bierce

LXXXV

Three animals on board a sinking ship prepared to take to the water. It was agreed among them that the bear should be lowered alongside; the mouse (who was to act as pilot) should embark upon him at once, to beat off the drowning sailors; and the monkey should follow, with provisions for the expedition—which arrangement was successfully carried out. The fourth day out from the wreck, the bear began to propound a series of leading questions concerning dinner; when it appeared that the monkey had provided but a single nut.

"I thought this would keep me awhile," he explained, "and you could eat the pilot."

Hearing this, the mouse vanished like a flash into the bear's ear, and fearing the hungry beast would then demand the nut, the monkey hastily devoured it. Not being in a position to insist upon his rights, the bear merely gobbled up the monkey.

LXXXVI

A lamb suffering from thirst went to a brook to drink. Putting his nose to the water, he was interested to feel it bitten by a fish. Not liking fish, he drew back and sought another place; but his persecutor getting there before him administered the same rebuff. The lamb being rather persevering, and the fish having no appointments for that day, this was repeated a few thousand times, when the former felt justified in swearing:

"I'm eternally boiled!" said he, "if ever I experienced so many fish in all my life. It is discouraging. It inspires me with mint sauce and green peas."

He probably meant amazement and fear; under the influence of powerful emotions even lambs will talk "shop."

"Well, good bye," said his tormentor, taking a final nip at the animal's muzzle; "I should like to amuse you some more; but I have other fish to fry."

This tale teaches a good quantity of lessons; but it does *not* teach why this fish should have persecuted this lamb.

Ambrose Bierce

A mole, in pursuing certain geological researches, came upon the buried carcase of a mule, and was about to tunnel him.

"Slow down, my good friend," said the deceased. "Push your mining operations in a less sacrilegious direction. Respect the dead, as you hope for death!"

"You have that about you," said the gnome, "that must make your grave respected in a certain sense, for at least such a period as your immortal part may require for perfect exhalation. The immunity I accord is not conceded to your sanctity, but extorted by your scent. The sepulchres of moles only are sacred."

To moles, the body of a lifeless mule A dead mule's carcase is, and nothing more.

LXXXVIII

"I think I'll set my sting into you, my obstructive friend," said a bee to an iron pump against which she had flown; "you are always more or less in the way."

"If you do," retorted the other, "I'll pump on you, if I can get any one to work my handle."

Exasperated by this impotent conservative threat, she pushed her little dart against him with all her vigour. When she tried to sheathe it again she couldn't, but she still made herself useful about the hive by hooking on to small articles and dragging them about. But no other bee would sleep with her after this; and so, by her ill-judged resentment, she was self-condemmed to a solitary cell.

The young reader may profitably beware.

Ambrose Bierce

LXXXIX

A Chinese dog, who had been much abroad with his master, was asked, upon his return, to state the most ludicrous fact he had observed.

"There is a country," said he, "the people of which are eternally speaking about 'Persian honesty,' 'Persian courage,' 'Persian loyalty,' 'Persian love of fair play,' &c., as if the Persians enjoyed a clear monopoly of these universal virtues. What is more, they speak thus in blind good faith—with a dense gravity of conviction that is simply amazing."

"But," urged the auditors, "we requested something ludicrous, not amazing."

"Exactly; the ludicrous part is the name of their country, which is—"

"What?"

"Persia."

XC

There was a calf, who, suspecting the purity of the milk supplied him by his dam, resolved to transfer his patronage to the barn-yard pump.

"Better," said he, "a pure article of water, than a diet that is neither fish, flesh, nor fowl."

But, although extremely regular in his new diet—taking it all the time—he did not seem to thrive as might have been expected. The larger orders he drew, the thinner and the more transparent he became; and at last, when the shadow of his person had become to him a vague and unreal memory, he repented, and applied to be reinstated in his comfortable sinecure at the maternal udder.

"Ah! my prodigal son," said the old lady, lowering her horns as if to permit him to weep upon her neck, "I regret that it is out of my power to celebrate your return by killing the fatted calf; but what I can I will do."

And she killed him instead.

Mot herl yaff ecti onk nocksal loth ervir tu esperfec tlyc old.[A]

[Footnote A: The learned reader will appreciate the motive which has prompted me to give this moral only in the original Persian.—TRANSLATOR.]

XCI

"There, now," said a kitten, triumphantly, laying a passive mouse at the feet of her mother. "I flatter myself I am coming on with a reasonable degree of rapidity. What will become of the minor quadrupeds when I have attained my full strength and ferocity, it is mournful to conjecture!"

"Did he give you much trouble?" inquired the aged ornament of the hearth-side, with a look of tender solicitude.

"Trouble!" echoed the kitten, "I never had such a fight in all my life! He was a downright savage—in his day."

"My Falstaffian issue," rejoined the Tabby, dropping her eyelids and composing her head for a quiet sleep, "the above is a *toy* mouse."

XCII

A crab who had travelled from the mouth of the Indus all the way to Ispahan, knocked, with much chuckling, at the door of the King's physician.

"Who's there?" shouted the doctor, from his divan within.

"A bad case of *cancer*," was the complacent reply.

"Good!" returned the doctor; "I'll *cure* you, my friend."

So saying, he conducted his facetious patient into the kitchen, and potted him in pickle. It cured him—of practical jocularity.

May the fable heal *you*, if you are afflicted with that form of evil.

XCIII

A certain magician owned a learned pig, who had lived a cleanly gentlemanly life, achieving great fame, and winning the hearts of all the people. But perceiving he was not happy, the magician, by a process easily explained did space permit, transformed him into a man. Straightway the creature abandoned his cards, his timepiece, his musical instruments, and all other devices of his profession, and betook him to a pool of mud, wherein he inhumed himself to the tip of his nose.

"Ten minutes ago," said the magician reprovingly, "you would have scorned to do an act like that."

"True," replied the biped, with a contented grunt; "I was then a learned pig; I am now a learned man."

"Nature has been very kind to her creatures," said a giraffe to an elephant. "For example, your neck being so very short, she has given you a proboscis wherewith to reach your food; and I having no proboscis, she has bestowed upon me a long neck."

"I think, my good friend, you have been among the theologians," said the elephant. "I doubt if I am clever enough to argue with you. I can only say it does not strike me that way."

"But, really," persisted the giraffe, "you must confess your trunk is a great convenience, in that it enables you to reach the high branches of which you are so fond, even as my long neck enables me."

"Perhaps," mused the ungrateful pachyderm, "if we could not reach the higher branches, we should develop a taste for the lower ones."

"In any case," was the rejoinder, "we can never be sufficiently thankful that we are unlike the lowly hippopotamus, who can reach neither the one nor the other."

"Ah! yes," the elephant assented, "there does not seem to have been enough of Nature's kindness to go round."

"But the hippopotamus has his roots and his rushes."

"It is not easy to see how, with his present appliances, he could obtain anything else."

This fable teaches nothing; for those who perceive the meaning of it either knew it before, or will not be taught.

Ambrose Bierce

XCV

A pious heathen who was currying favour with his wooden deity by sitting for some years motionless in a treeless plain, observed a young ivy putting forth her tender shoots at his feet. He thought he could endure the additional martyrdom of a little shade, and begged her to make herself quite at home.

"Exactly," said the plant; "it is my mission to adorn venerable ruins."

She lapped her clinging tendrils about his wasted shanks, and in six months had mantled him in green.

"It is now time," said the devotee, a year later, "for me to fulfil the remainder of my religious vow. I must put in a few seasons of howling and leaping. You have been very good, but I no longer require your gentle ministrations."

"But I require yours," replied the vine; "you have become a second nature to me. Let others indulge in the delights of gymnastic worship; you and I will 'surfer and be strong' —respectively."

The devotee muttered something about the division of labour, and his bones are still pointed out to the pilgrim.

XCVI

A fox seeing a swan afloat, called out:

"What ship is that? I wish to take passage by your line."

"Got a ticket?" inquired the fowl.

"No; I'll make it all right with the company, though."

So the swan moored alongside, and he embarked,—deck passage. When they were well off shore the fox intimated that dinner would be agreeable.

"I would advise you not to try the ship's provisions," said the bird; "we have only salt meat on board. Beware the scurvy!"

"You are quite right," replied the passenger; "I'll see if I can stay my stomach with the foremast."

So saying he bit off her neck, and she immediately capsizing, he was drowned.

MORAL—highly so, but not instructive.

Ambrose Bierce

XCVII

A monkey finding a heap of cocoa-nuts, gnawed into one, then dropped it, gagging hideously.

"Now, this is what *I* call perfectly disgusting!" said he: "I can never leave anything lying about but some one comes along and puts a quantity of nasty milk into it!"

A cat just then happening to pass that way began rolling the cocoa-nuts about with her paw.

"Yeow!" she exclaimed; "it is enough to vex the soul of a cast-iron dog! Whenever I set out any milk to cool, somebody comes and seals it up tight as a drum!"

Then perceiving one another, and each thinking the other the offender, these enraged animals contended, and wrought a mutual extermination. Whereby two worthy consumers were lost to society, and a quantity of excellent food had to be given to the poor.

XCVIII

A mouse who had overturned an earthern jar was discovered by a cat, who entered from an adjoining room and began to upbraid him in the harshest and most threatening manner.

"You little wretch!" said she, "how dare you knock over that valuable urn? If it had been filled with hot water, and I had been lying before it asleep, I should have been scalded to death."

"If it had been full of water," pleaded the mouse, "it would not have upset."

"But I might have lain down in it, monster!" persisted the cat.

"No, you couldn't," was the answer; "it is not wide enough."

"Fiend!" shrieked the cat, smashing him with her paw; "I can curl up real small when I try."

The *ultima ratio* of very angry people is frequently addressed to the ear of the dead.

Ambrose Bierce

XCIX

In crossing a frozen pool, a monkey slipped and fell, striking upon the back of his head with considerable force, so that the ice was very much shattered. A peacock, who was strutting about on shore thinking what a pretty peacock he was, laughed immoderately at the mishap. N.B.—All laughter is immoderate when a fellow is hurt—if the fellow is oneself.

"Bah!" exclaimed the sufferer; "if you could see the beautiful prismatic tints I have knocked into this ice, you would laugh out of the other side of your bill. The splendour of your tail is quite eclipsed."

Thus craftily did he inveigle the vain bird, who finally came and spread his tail alongside the fracture for comparison. The gorgeous feathers at once froze fast to the ice, and—in short, that artless fowl passed a very uncomfortable winter.

C

A volcano, having discharged a few million tons of stones upon a small village, asked the mayor if he thought that a tolerably good supply for building purposes.

"I think," replied that functionary, "if you give us another dash of granite, and just a pinch of old red sandstone, we could manage with what you have already done for us. We would, however, be grateful for the loan of your crater to bake bricks."

"Oh, certainly; parties served at their residences." Then, after the man had gone, the mountain added, with mingled lava and contempt: "The most insatiable people I ever contracted to supply. They shall not have another pebble!"

He banked his fires, and in six weeks was as cold as a neglected pudding. Then might you have seen the heaving of the surface boulders, as the people began stirring forty fathoms beneath.

When you have got quite enough of anything, make it manifest by asking for some more. You won't get it.

CI

"I entertain for you a sentiment of profound amity," said the tiger to the leopard. "And why should I not? for are we not members of the same great feline family?"

"True," replied the leopard, who was engaged in the hopeless endeavour to change his spots; "since we have mutually plundered one another's hunting grounds of everything edible, there remains no grievance to quarrel about. You are a good fellow; let us embrace!"

They did so with the utmost heartiness; which being observed by a contiguous monkey, that animal got up a tree, where he delivered himself of the wisdom following:

"There is nothing so touching as these expressions of mutual regard between animals who are vulgarly believed to hate one another. They render the brief intervals of peace almost endurable to both parties. But the difficulty is, there are so many excellent reasons why these relatives should live in peace, that they won't have time to state them all before the next fight."

A woodpecker, who had bored a multitude of holes in the body of a dead tree, was asked by a robin to explain their purpose.

"As yet, in the infancy of science," replied the woodpecker, "I am quite unable to do so. Some naturalists affirm that I hide acorns in these pits; others maintain that I get worms out of them. I endeavoured for some time to reconcile the two theories; but the worms ate my acorns, and then would not come out. Since then, I have left science to work out its own problems, while I work out the holes. I hope the final decision may be in some way advantageous to me; for at my nest I have a number of prepared holes which I can hammer into some suitable tree at a moment's notice. Perhaps I could insert a few into the scientific head."

"No-o-o," said the robin, reflectively, "I should think not. A prepared hole is an idea; I don't think it could get in."

MORAL.—It might be driven in with a steam-hammer.

Ambrose Bierce

CIII

"Are you going to this great hop?" inquired a spruce cricket of a labouring beetle.

"No," replied he, sadly, "I've got to attend this great ball."

"Blest if I know the difference," drawled a more offensive insect, with his head in an empty silk hat; "and I've been in society all my life. But why was I not invited to either hop or ball?"

He is now invited to the latter.

CIV

"Too bad, too bad," said a young Abyssinian to a yawning hippopotamus.

"What is 'too bad?'" inquired the quadruped. "What is the matter with you?"

"Oh, *I* never complain," was the reply; "I was only thinking of the niggard economy of Nature in building a great big beast like you and not giving him any mouth."

"H'm, h'm! it was still worse," mused the beast, "to construct a great wit like you and give him no seasonable occasion for the display of his cleverness."

A moment later there were a cracking of bitten bones, a great gush of animal fluids, the vanishing of two black feet—in short, the fatal poisoning of an indiscreet hippopotamus.

The rubbing of a bit of lemon about the beaker's brim is the finishing-touch to a whiskey punch. Much misery may be thus averted.

CV

A salmon vainly attempted to leap up a cascade. After trying a few thousand times, he grew so fatigued that he began to leap less and think more. Suddenly an obvious method of surmounting the difficulty presented itself to the salmonic intelligence.

"Strange," he soliloquized, as well as he could in the water, —"very strange I did not think of it before! I'll go above the fall and leap downwards."

So he went out on the bank, walked round to the upper side of the fall, and found he could leap over quite easily. Ever afterwards when he went up-stream in the spring to be caught, he adopted this plan. He has been heard to remark that the price of salmon might be brought down to a merely nominal figure, if so many would not wear themselves out before getting up to where there is good fishing.

CVI

"The son of a jackass," shrieked a haughty mare to a mule who had offended her by expressing an opinion, "should cultivate the simple grace of intellectual humility."

"It is true," was the meek reply, "I cannot boast an illustrious ancestry; but at least I shall never be called upon to blush for my posterity. Yonder mule colt is as proper a son—"

"Yonder mule colt?" interrupted the mare, with a look of ineffable contempt for her auditor; "that is *my* colt!"

"The consort of a jackass and the mother of mules," retorted he, quietly, "should cultivate the simple thingamy of intellectual whatsitsname."

The mare muttered something about having some shopping to do, threw on her harness, and went out to call a cab.

Ambrose Bierce

"Hi! hi!" squeaked a pig, running after a hen who had just left her nest; "I say, mum, you dropped this 'ere. It looks wal'able; which I fetched it along!" And splitting his long face, he laid a warm egg at her feet.

"You meddlesome bacon!" cackled the ungrateful bird; "if you don't take that orb directly back, I 'll sit on you till I hatch you out of your saddle-cover!"

MORAL.—Virtue is its only reward.

CVIII

A rustic, preparing to devour an apple, was addressed by a brace of crafty and covetous birds:

"Nice apple that," said one, critically examining it. "I don't wish to disparage it—wouldn't say a word against that vegetable for all the world. But I never can look upon an apple of that variety without thinking of my poisoned nestling! Ah! so plump, and rosy, and—rotten!"

"Just so," said the other. "And you remember my good father, who perished in that orchard. Strange that so fair a skin should cover so vile a heart!"

Just then another fowl came flying up.

"I came in, all haste," said he, "to warn you about that fruit. My late lamented wife ate some off the same tree. Alas! how comely to the eye, and how essentially noxious!"

"I am very grateful," the young man said; "but I am unable to comprehend how the sight of this pretty piece of painted confectionery should incite you all to slander your dead relations."

Whereat there was confusion in the demeanour of that feathered trio.

Ambrose Bierce

CIX

"The Millennium is come," said a lion to a lamb. "Suppose you come out of that fold, and let us lie down together, as it has been foretold we should."

"Been to dinner to-day?" inquired the lamb.

"Not a bite of anything since breakfast," was the reply, "except a few lean swine, a saddle or two, and some old harness."

"I distrust a Millennium," continued the lamb, thoughtfully, "which consists *solely* in our lying down together. My notion of that happy time is that it is a period in which pork and leather are not articles of diet, but in which every respectable lion shall have as much mutton as he can consume. However, you may go over to yonder sunny hill and lie down until I come."

It is singular how a feeling of security tends to develop cunning. If that lamb had been out upon the open plain he would have readily fallen into the snare—and it was studded very thickly with teeth.

CX

"I say, you!" bawled a fat ox in a stall to a lusty young ass who was braying outside; "the like of that is not in good taste!"

"In whose good taste, my adipose censor?" inquired the ass, not too respectfully.

"Why—h'm—ah! I mean it does not suit *me*. You ought to bellow."

"May I inquire how it happens to be any of your business whether I bellow or bray, or do both—or neither?"

"I cannot tell you," answered the critic, shaking his head despondingly; "I do not at all understand it. I can only say that I have been accustomed to censure all discourse that differs from my own."

"Exactly," said the ass; "you have sought to make an art of impertinence by mistaking preferences for principles. In 'taste' you have invented a word incapable of definition, to denote an idea impossible of expression; and by employing in connection therewith the words 'good' and 'bad,' you indicate a merely subjective process in terms of an objective quality. Such presumption transcends the limit of the merely impudent, and passes into the boundless empyrean of pure cheek!"

At the close of this remarkable harangue, the bovine critic was at a loss for language to express his disapproval. So he said the speech was in bad taste.

CXI

A bloated toad, studded with dermal excrescences, was boasting that she was the wartiest creature alive.

"Perhaps you are," said her auditor, emerging from the soil; "but it is a barren and superficial honour. Look at me: I am one solid mole!"

CXII

"It is very difficult getting on in the world," sighed a weary snail; "very difficult indeed, with such high rents!"

"You don't mean to say you pay anything for that old rookery!" said a slug, who was characteristically insinuating himself between the stems of the celery intended for dinner. "A miserable old shanty like that, without stables, grounds, or any modern conveniences!"

"Pay!" said the snail, contemptuously; "I'd like to see you get a semi-detatched villa like this at a nominal rate!"

"Why don't you let your upper apartments to a respectable single party?" urged the slug.

The answer is not recorded.

Ambrose Bierce

CXIII

A hare, pursued by a dog, sought sanctuary in the den of a wolf. It being after business hours, the latter was at home to him.

"Ah!" panted the hare; "how very fortunate! I feel quite safe here, for you dislike dogs quite as much as I do."

"Your security, my small friend," replied the wolf, "depends not upon those points in which you and I agree, but upon those in which I and the dog differ."

"Then you mean to eat me?" inquired the timorous puss.

"No-o-o," drawled the wolf, reflectively, "I should not like to promise *that*; I mean to eat a part of you. There may be a tuft of fur, and a toe-nail or two, left for you to go on with. I am hungry, but I am not hoggish."

"The distinction is too fine for me," said the hare, scratching her head.

"That, my friend, is because you have not made a practice of hare-splitting. I have."

CXIV

"Oyster at home?" inquired a monkey, rapping at the closed shell.

There was no reply. Dropping the knocker, he laid hold of the bell-handle, ringing a loud peal, but without effect.

"Hum, hum!" he mused, with a look of disappointment, "gone to the sea side, I suppose."

So he turned away, thinking he would call again later in the season; but he had not proceeded far before he conceived a brilliant idea. Perhaps there had been a suicide!—or a murder! He would go back and force the door. By way of doing so he obtained a large stone, and smashed in the roof. There had been no murder to justify such audacity, so he committed one.

The funeral was gorgeous. There were mute oysters with wands, drunken oysters with scarves and hat-bands, a sable hearse with hearth-dusters on it, a swindling undertaker's bill, and all the accessories of a first-rate churchyard circus—everything necessary but the corpse. That had been disposed of by the monkey, and the undertaker meanly withheld the use of his own.

MORAL.—A lamb foaled in March makes the best pork when his horns have attained the length of an inch.

Ambrose Bierce

CXV

"Pray walk into my parlour," said the spider to the fly.
"That is not quite original," the latter made reply.
"If that's the way you plagiarize, your fame will be a fib—
But I'll walk into your parlour, while I pitch into your crib.
But before I cross your threshold, sir, if I may make so free,
Pray let me introduce to you my friend, 'the wicked flea.'"
"How do you?" says the spider, as his welcome he extends;
"'How doth the busy little bee,' and all our other friends?"
"Quite well, I think, and quite unchanged," the flea said;
"though I learn,
In certain quarters well informed, 'tis feared 'the worm will
turn.'"
"Humph!" said the fly; "I do not understand this talk—
not I!"
"It is 'classical allusion,'" said the spider to the fly.

CXVI

A polar bear navigating the mid-sea upon the mortal part of a late lamented walrus, soliloquized, in substance, as follows:

"Such liberty of action as I am afflicted with is enough to embarrass any bear that ever bore. I can remain passive, and starve; or I can devour my ship, and drown. I am really unable to decide."

So he sat down to think it over. He considered the question in all its aspects, until he grew quite thin; turned it over and over in his mind until he was too weak to sit up; meditated upon it with a constantly decreasing pulse, a rapidly failing respiration. But he could not make up his mind, and finally expired without having come to a decision.

It appears to me he might almost as well have chosen starvation, at a venture.

Ambrose Bierce

CXVII

A sword-fish having penetrated seven or eight feet into the bottom of a ship, under the impression that he was quarrelling with a whale, was unable to draw out of the fight. The sailors annoyed him a good deal, by pounding with handspikes upon that portion of his horn inside; but he bore it as bravely as he could, putting the best possible face upon the matter, until he saw a shark swimming by, of whom he inquired the probable destination of the ship.

"Italy, I think," said the other, grinning. "I have private reasons for believing her cargo consists mainly of consumptives."

"Ah!" exclaimed the captive; "Italy, delightful clime of the cerulean orange—the rosy olive! Land of the night-blooming Jesuit, and the fragrant *laszarone*! It would be heavenly to run down gondolas in the streets of Venice! I *must* go to Italy."

"Indeed you must," said the shark, darting suddenly aft, where he had caught the gleam of shotted canvas through the blue waters.

But it was fated to be otherwise: some days afterwards the ship and fish passed over a sunken rock which almost grazed the keel. Then the two parted company, with mutual expressions of tender regard, and a report which could be traced by those on board to no trustworthy source.

The foregoing fable shows that a man of good behaviour need not care for money, and *vice versa*.

CXVIII

A facetious old cat seeing her kitten sleeping in a bath tub, went down into the cellar and turned on the hot water. (For the convenience of the bathers the bath was arranged in that way; you had to undress, and then go down to the cellar to let on the wet.) No sooner did the kitten remark the unfamiliar sensation, than he departed thence with a willingness quite creditable in one who was not a professional acrobat, and met his mother on the kitchen stairs.

"Aha! my steaming hearty!" cried the elder grimalkin; "I coveted you when I saw the cook put you in the dinner-pot. If I have a weakness, it is hare—hare nicely dressed, and partially boiled."

Whereupon she made a banquet of her suffering offspring.[A]

Adversity works a stupendous change in tender youth; many a young man is never recognized by his parents after having been in hot water.

[Footnote A: Here should have followed the appropriate and obvious classical allusion. It is known our fabulist was classically educated. Why, then, this disgraceful omission?—TRANSLATOR.]

Ambrose Bierce

CXIX

"It is a waste of valour for us to do battle," said a lame ostrich to a negro who had suddenly come upon her in the desert; "let us cast lots to see who shall be considered the victor, and then go about our business."

To this proposition the negro readily assented. They cast lots: the negro cast lots of stones, and the ostrich cast lots of feathers. Then the former went about his business, which consisted of skinning the bird.

MORAL.—There is nothing like the arbitrament of chance. That form of it known as *trile-bi-joorie* is perhaps as good as any.

CXX

An author who had wrought a book of fables (the merit whereof transcended expression) was peacefully sleeping atop of the modest eminence to which he had attained, when he was rudely awakened by a throng of critics, emitting adverse judgment upon the tales he had builded.

"Apparently," said he, "I have been guilty of some small grains of unconsidered wisdom, and the same have proven a bitterness to these excellent folk, the which they will not abide. Ah, well! those who produce the Strasburg *pate* and the feather-pillow are prone to regard *us* as rival creators. I presume it is in course of nature for him who grows the pen to censure the manner of its use."

So speaking, he executed a smile a hand's-breadth in extent, and resumed his airy dream of dropping ducats.

Ambrose Bierce

CXXI

For many years an opossum had anointed his tail with bear's oil, but it remained stubbornly bald-headed. At last his patience was exhausted, and he appealed to Bruin himself, accusing him of breaking faith, and calling him a quack.

"Why, you insolent marsupial!" retorted the bear in a rage; "you expect my oil to give you hair upon your tail, when it will not give me even a tail. Why don't you try under-draining, or top-dressing with light compost?"

They said and did a good deal more before the opossum withdrew his cold and barren member from consideration; but the judicious fabulist does not encumber his tale with extraneous matter, lest it be pointless.

CXXII

"So disreputable a lot as you are I never saw!" said a sleepy rat to the casks in a wine-cellar. "Always making night hideous with your hoops and hollows, and disfiguring the day with your bunged-up appearance. There is no sleeping when once the wine has got into your heads. I'll report you to the butler!"

"The sneaking tale-bearer," said the casks. "Let us beat him with our staves."

"*Requiescat in pace*," muttered a learned cobweb, sententiously.

"Requires a cat in the place, does it?" shrieked the rat. "Then I'm off!"

To explain all the wisdom imparted by this fable would require the pen of a pig, and volumes of smoke.

CXXIII

A giraffe having trodden upon the tail of a poodle, that animal flew into a blind rage, and wrestled valorously with the invading foot.

"Hullo, sonny!" said the giraffe, looking down, "what are you doing there?"

"I am fighting!" was the proud reply; "but I don't know that it is any of your business."

"Oh, I have no desire to mix in," said the good-natured giraffe. "I never take sides in terrestrial strife. Still, as that is my foot, I think—"

"Eh!" cried the poodle, backing some distance away and gazing upward, shading his eyes with his paw. "You don't mean to say—by Jove it's a fact! Well, that beats *me*! A beast of such enormous length—such preposterous duration, as it were—I wouldn't have believed it! Of course I can't quarrel with a non-resident; but why don't you have a local agent on the ground?"

The reply was probably the wisest ever made; but it has not descended to this generation. It had so very far to descend.

CXXIV

A dog having got upon the scent of a deer which a hunter had been dragging home, set off with extraordinary zeal. After measuring off a few leagues, he paused.

"My running gear is all right," said he; "but I seem to have lost my voice."

Suddenly his ear was assailed by a succession of eager barks, as of another dog in pursuit of him. It then began to dawn upon him that he was a particularly rapid dog: instead of having lost his voice, his voice had lost him, and was just now arriving. Full of his discovery, he sought his master, and struck for better food and more comfortable housing.

"Why, you miserable example of perverted powers!" said his master; "I never intended you for the chase, but for the road. You are to be a draught-dog—to pull baby about in a cart. You will perceive that speed is an objection. Sir, you must be toned down; you will be at once assigned to a house with modern conveniences, and will dine at a French restaurant. If that system do not reduce your own, I'm an 'Ebrew Jew!"

The journals next morning had racy and appetizing accounts of a canine suicide.

Ambrose Bierce

CXXV

A gosling, who had not yet begun to blanch, was accosted by a chicken just out of the shell:

"Whither away so fast, fair maid?" inquired the chick.

"Wither away yourself," was the contemptuous reply; "you are already in the sere and yellow leaf; while I seem to have a green old age before me."

CXXVI

A famishing traveller who had run down a salamander, made a fire, and laid him alive upon the hot coals to cook. Wearied with the pursuit which had preceded his capture, the animal at once composed himself, and fell into a refreshing sleep. At the end of a half-hour, the man, stirred him with a stick, remarking:

"I say!—wake up and begin toasting, will you? How long do you mean to keep dinner waiting, eh?"

"Oh, I beg you will not wait for me," was the yawning reply. "If you are going to stand upon ceremony, everything will get cold. Besides, I have dined. I wish, by-the-way, you would put on some more fuel; I think we shall have snow."

"Yes," said the man, "the weather is like yourself—raw, and exasperatingly cool. Perhaps this will warm you." And he rolled a ponderous pine log atop of that provoking reptile, who flattened out, and "handed in his checks."

> The moral thus doth glibly run—
> A cause its opposite may brew;
> The sun-shade is unlike the sun,
> The plum unlike the plumber, too.
> A salamander underdone
> His impudence may overdo.

CXXVII

A humming-bird invited a vulture to dine with her. He accepted, but took the precaution to have an emetic along with him; and immediately after dinner, which consisted mainly of dew, spices, honey, and similar slops, he swallowed his corrective, and tumbled the distasteful viands out. He then went away, and made a good wholesome meal with his friend the ghoul. He has been heard to remark, that the taste for humming-bird fare is "too artificial for *him*." He says, a simple and natural diet, with agreeable companions, cheerful surroundings, and a struggling moon, is best for the health, and most agreeable to the normal palate.

People with vitiated tastes may derive much profit from this opinion. *Crede experto.*

CXXVIII

A certain terrier, of a dogmatic turn, asked a kitten her opinion of rats, demanding a categorical answer. The opinion, as given, did not possess the merit of coinciding with his own; whereupon he fell upon the heretic and bit her—bit her until his teeth were much worn and her body much elongated—bit her good! Having thus vindicated the correctness of his own view, he felt so amiable a satisfaction that he announced his willingness to adopt the opinion of which he had demonstrated the harmlessness. So he begged his enfeebled antagonist to re-state it, which she incautiously did. No sooner, however, had the superior debater heard it for the second time than he resumed his intolerance, and made an end of that unhappy cat.

"Heresy," said he, wiping his mouth, "may be endured in the vigorous and lusty; but in a person lying at the very point of death such hardihood is intolerable."

It is always intolerable.

Ambrose Bierce

CXXIX

A tortoise and an armadillo quarrelled, and agreed to fight it out. Repairing to a secluded valley, they put themselves into hostile array.

"Now come on!" shouted the tortoise, shrinking into the inmost recesses of his shell.

"All right," shrieked the armadillo, coiling up tightly in his coat of mail; "I am ready for you!"

And thus these heroes waged the awful fray from morn till dewy eve, at less than a yard's distance. There has never been anything like it; their endurance was something marvellous! During the night each combatant sneaked silently away; and the historian of the period obscurely alludes to the battle as "the naval engagement of the future."

CXXX

Two hedgehogs having conceived a dislike to a hare, conspired for his extinction. It was agreed between them that the lighter and more agile of the two should beat him up, surround him, run him into a ditch, and drive him upon the thorns of the more gouty and unwieldy conspirator. It was not a very hopeful scheme, but it was the best they could devise. There was a chance of success if the hare should prove willing, and, gambler-like, they decided to take that chance, instead of trusting to the remote certainty of their victim's death from natural cause. The doomed animal performed his part as well as could be reasonably expected of him: every time the enemy's flying detachment pressed him hard, he fled playfully toward the main body, and lightly vaulted over, about eight feet above the spines. And this prickly blockhead had not the practical sagacity to get upon a wall seven feet and six inches high!

This fable is designed to show that the most desperate chances are comparatively safe.

Ambrose Bierce

CXXXI

A young eel inhabiting the mouth of a river in India, determined to travel. Being a fresh-water eel, he was somewhat restricted in his choice of a route, but he set out with a cheerful heart and very little luggage. Before he had proceeded very far up-stream he found the current too strong to be overcome without a ruinous consumption of coals. He decided to anchor his tail where it then was, and *grow* up. For the first hundred miles it was tolerably tedious work, but when he had learned to tame his impatience, he found this method of progress rather pleasant than otherwise. But when he began to be caught at widely separate points by the fishermen of eight or ten different nations, he did not think it so fine.

This fable teaches that when you extend your residence you multiply your experiences. A local eel can know but little of angling.

CXXXII

Some of the lower animals held a convention to settle for ever the unspeakably important question, What is Life?

"Life," squeaked the poet, blinking and folding his filmy wings, "is—." His kind having been already very numerously heard from upon the subject, he was choked off.

"Life," said the scientist, in a voice smothered by the earth he was throwing up into small hills, "is the harmonious action of heterogeneous but related faculties, operating in accordance with certain natural laws."

"Ah!" chattered the lover, "but that thawt of thing is vewy gweat blith in the thothiety of one'th thweetheart." And curling his tail about a branch, he swung himself heavenward and had a spasm.

"It is *vita!*" grunted the sententious scholar, pausing in his mastication of a Chaldaic root.

"It is a thistle," brayed the warrior: "very nice thing to take!"

"Life, my friends," croaked the philosopher from his hollow tree, dropping the lids over his cattish eyes, "is a disease. We are all symptoms."

"Pooh!" ejaculated the physician, uncoiling and springing his rattle. "How then does it happen that when *we* remove the symptoms, the disease is gone?"

"I would give something to know that," replied the philosopher, musingly; "but I suspect that in most cases the inflammation remains, and is intensified."

Draw your own moral inference, "in your own jugs."

Ambrose Bierce

CXXXIII

A heedless boy having flung a pebble in the direction of a basking lizard, that reptile's tail disengaged itself, and flew some distance away. One of the properties of a lizard's camp-follower is to leave the main body at the slightest intimation of danger.

"There goes that vexatious narrative again," exclaimed the lizard, pettishly; "I never had such a tail in my life! Its restless tendency to divorce upon insufficient grounds is enough to harrow the reptilian soul! Now," he continued, backing up to the fugitive part, "perhaps you will be good enough to resume your connection with the parent establishment."

No sooner was the splice effected, than an astronomer passing that way casually remarked to a friend that he had just sighted a comet. Supposing itself menaced, the timorous member again sprang away, coming down plump before the horny nose of a sparrow. Here its career terminated.

We sometimes escape from an imaginary danger, only to find some real persecutor has a little bill against us.

CXXXIV

A jackal who had pursued a deer all day with unflagging industry, was about to seize him, when an earthquake, which was doing a little civil engineering in that part of the country, opened a broad chasm between him and his prey.

"Now, here," said he, "is a distinct interference with the laws of nature. But if we are to tolerate miracles, there is an end of all progress."

So speaking, he endeavoured to cross the abyss at two jumps. His fate would serve the purpose of an impressive warning if it might be clearly ascertained; but the earth having immediately pinched together again, the research of the moral investigator is baffled.

Ambrose Bierce

CXXXV

"Ah!" sighed a three-legged stool, "if I had only been a quadruped, I should have been happy as the day is long—which, on the twenty-first of June, would be considerable felicity for a stool."

"Ha! look at me!" said a toadstool; "consider my superior privation, and be content with your comparatively happy lot."

"I don't discern," replied the first, "how the contemplation of unipedal misery tends to alleviate tripedal wretchedness."

"You don't, eh!" sneered the toadstool. "You mean, do you, to fly in the face of all the moral and social philosophers?"

"Not unless some benefactor of his race shall impel me."

"H'm! I think Zambri the Parsee is the man for that kindly office, my dear."

This final fable teaches that he is.

BRIEF SEASONS OF INTELLECTUAL DISSIPATION

I

FOOL.—I have a question for you.

PHILOSOPHER.—I have a number of them for myself. Do you happen to have heard that a fool can ask more questions in a breath than a philosopher can answer in a life?

F.—I happen to have heard that in such a case the one is as great a fool as the other.

PH.—Then there is no distinction between folly and philosophy?

F.—Don't lay the flattering unction to your soul. The province of folly is to ask unanswerable questions. It is the function of philosophy to answer them.

PH.—Admirable fool!

F.—Am I? Pray tell me the meaning of "a fool."

PH.—Commonly he has none.

F.—I mean—

PH.—Then in this case he has one.

F.—I lick thy boots! But what does Solomon indicate by the word fool? That is what I mean.

PH.—Let us then congratulate Solomon upon the agreement between the views of you two. However, I twig your intent: he means a wicked sinner; and of all forms of folly there is none so great as wicked sinning. For goodness is, in the end, more conducive to personal happiness—which is the sole aim of man.

F.—Hath virtue no better excuse than this?

PH.—Possibly; philosophy is not omniscience.

F.—Instructed I sit at thy feet!

PH.—Unwilling to instruct, I stand on my head.

* * * * *

FOOL.—You say personal happiness is the sole aim of man.

PHILOSOPHER.—Then it is.

F.—But this is much disputed.

PH.—There is much personal happiness in disputation.

F.—Socrates—

PH.—Hold! I detest foreigners.

F.—Wisdom, they say, is of no country.

PH.—Of none that I have seen.

* * * * *

FOOL.—Let us return to our subject—the sole aim of

mankind. Crack me these nuts. (1) The man, never weary of well-doing, who endures a life of privation for the good of his fellow-creatures?

PHILOSOPHER.—Does he feel remorse in so doing? or does the rascal rather like it?

F.—(2) He, then, who, famishing himself, parts his loaf with a beggar?

PH.—There are people who prefer benevolence to bread.

F.—Ah! *De gustibus*—

PH.—Shut up!

F.—Well, (3) how of him who goes joyfully to martyrdom?

PH.—He goes joyfully.

F.—And yet—

PH.—Did you ever converse with a good man going to the stake?

F.—I never saw a good man going to the stake.

PH.—Unhappy pupil! you were born some centuries too early.

*　*　*　*　*

FOOL.—You say you detest foreigners. Why?

PHILOSOPHER.—Because I am human.

F.—But so are they.

PH.—Excellent fool! I thank thee for the better reason.

PHILOSOPHER.—I have been thinking of the *pocopo*.

FOOL.—Is it open to the public?

PH.—The pocopo is a small animal of North America, chiefly remarkable for singularity of diet. It subsists solely upon a single article of food.

F.—What is that?

PH.—Other pocopos. Unable to obtain this, their natural sustenance, a great number of pocopos die annually of starvation. Their death leaves fewer mouths to feed, and by consequence their race is rapidly multiplying.

F.—From whom had you this?

PH.—A professor of political economy.

F.—I bend in reverence! What made you think of the pocopo?

PH.—Speaking of man.

F.—If you did not wish to think of the pocopo, and speaking of man would make you think of it, you would not speak of man, would you?

PH.—Certainly not.

F.—Why not?

PH.—I do not know.

F.—Excellent philosopher!

*   *   *   *   *

FOOL.—I have attentively considered your teachings. They may be full of wisdom; they are certainly out of taste.

PHILOSOPHER.—Whose taste?

F.—Why, that of people of culture.

PH.—Do any of these people chance to have a taste for intoxication, tobacco, hard hats, false hair, the nude ballet, and over-feeding?

F.—Possibly; but in intellectual matters you must confess their taste is correct.

PH.—Why must I?

F.—They say so themselves.

*　　*　　*　　*　　*

PHILOSOPHER.—I have been thinking why a dolt is called a donkey.

FOOL.—I had thought philosophy concerned itself with a less personal class of questions; but why is it?

PH.—The essential quality of a dolt is stupidity.

F.—Mine ears are drunken!

PH.—The essential quality of an ass is asininity.

F.—Divine philosophy!

PH.—As commonly employed, "stupidity" and "asininity" are convertible terms.

F.—That I, unworthy, should have lived to see this day!

II

FOOL.—If *I* were a doctor—

DOCTOR.—I should endeavour to be a fool.

F.—You would fail; folly is not easily achieved.

D.—True; man is overworked.

F.—Let him take a pill.

D.—If he like. I would not.

F.—You are too frank: take a fool's advice.

D.—Thank thee for the nastier prescription.

* * * * *

FOOL.—I have a friend who—

DOCTOR.—Stands in great need of my assistance. Absence of excitement, gentle restraint, a hard bed, simple diet—that will straighten him out.

F.—I'll give thee sixpence to let me touch the hem of thy garment!

D.—What of your friend?

F.—He is a gentleman.

D.—Then he is dead!

F.—Just so: he is "straightened out"—he took your prescription.

D.—All but the "simple diet."

F.—He is himself the diet.

D.—How simple!

* * * * *

FOOL.—Believe you a man retains his intellect after decapitation?

DOCTOR.—It is possible that he acquires it?

F.—Much good it does him.

D.—Why not—as compensation? He is at some disadvantage in other respects.

F.—For example?

D.—He is in a false position.

* * * * *

FOOL.—What is the most satisfactory disease?

DOCTOR.—Paralysis of the thoracic duct.

F.—I am not familiar with it.

D.—It does not encourage familiarity. Paralysis of the thoracic duct enables the patient to accept as many invitations to dinner as he can secure, without danger of spoiling his appetite.

F.—But how long does his appetite last?

D.—That depends. Always a trifle longer than he does.

F.—The portion that survives him—?

D.—Goes to swell the Mighty Gastric Passion which lurks darkly Outside, yawning to swallow up material creation!

F.—Pitch it a biscuit.

* * * * *

FOOL.—You attend a patient. He gets well. Good! How do you tell whether his recovery is because of your treatment or in spite of it?

DOCTOR.—I never do tell.

F.—I mean how do you know?

D.—I take the opinion of a person interested in the question: I ask a fool.

F.—How does the patient know?

D.—The fool asks me.

F.—Amiable instructor! How shall I reward thee?

D.—Eat a cucumber cut up in shilling claret.

* * * * *

DOCTOR.—The relation between a patient and his disease is the same as that which obtains between the two wooden weather-prophets of a Dutch clock. When the disease goes off, the patient goes on; when the disease goes on, the patient goes off.

FOOL.—A pauper conceit. Their relations, then, are not of the most cordial character.

D.—One's relations—except the poorer sort—seldom are.

F.—My tympanum is smitten with pleasant peltings of wisdom! I 'll lay you ten to one you cannot tell me the present condition of your last patient.

D.—Done!

F.—You have won the wager.

FOOL.—I once read the report of an actual conversation upon a scientific subject between a fool and a physician.

DOCTOR.—Indeed! That sort of conversation commonly takes place between fools only.

F.—The reporter had chosen to confound orthography: he spelt fool "phool," and physician "fysician." What the fool said was, therefore, preceded by "PH;" the remarks of the physician were indicated by the letter "F."

D.—This must have been very confusing.

F.—It was. But no one discovered that any liberties had been taken with orthography.

D.—You tumour!

*   *   *   *   *

FOOL.—Suppose you had amongst your menials an ailing oyster?

DOCTOR.—Oysters do not ail.

F.—I have heard that the pearl is the result of a disease.

D.—Whether a functional derangement producing a valuable gem can be properly termed, or treated as, a disease, is open to honest doubt.

F.—Then in the case supposed you would not favour excision of the abnormal part?

D.—Yes; I would remove the oyster.

F.—But if the pearl were growing very rapidly this operation would not be immediately advisable.

D.—That would depend upon the symptomatic diagnosis.

F.—Beast! Give me air!

* * * * *

DOCTOR.—I have been thinking—

FOOL.—(Liar!)

D.—That you "come out" rather well for a fool.

Can it be that I have been entertaining an angel unawares?

F.—Dismiss the apprehension: I am as great a fool as yourself. But there is a way by which in future you may resolve a similar doubt.

D.—Explain.

F.—Speak to your guest of symptomatic diagnosis. If he is an angel, he will not resent it.

III

SOLDIER (*reading from "Napier"*).—"Who would not rather be buried by an army upon the field of battle than by a sexton in a church-yard!"

FOOL.—I give it up.

S.—I am not aware that any one has asked you for an opinion.

F.—I am not aware that I have given one: there is a happiness yet in store for you.

S.—I will revel in anticipation.

F.—You must revel somehow; without revelry there would be no soldiering.

S.—Idiot.

F.—I beg your pardon: I had thought your profession had at least taught you to call people by their proper titles. In the service of mankind I hold the rank of Fool.

S.—What, ho! without there! Let the trumpets sound!

F.—I beg you will not.

S.—True; you beg: I will not.

F.—But why rob when stealing is more honourable?

S.—Consider the competition.

* * * * *

FOOL.—Sir Cut-throat, how many orphans have you made to-day?

Ambrose Bierce

SOLDIER.—The devil an orphan! Have you a family?

F.—Put up your iron; I am the last of my race.

S.—How? No more fools?

F.—Not one, so help me! They have all gone to the wars.

S.—And why, pray, have *you* not enlisted?

F.—I should be no fool if I knew.

*   *   *   *   *

FOOL.—You are somewhat indebted to me.

SOLDIER.—I do not acknowledge your claim. Let us submit the matter to arbitration.

F.—The only arbiter whose decision you respect is on your own side.

S.—You allude to my sword, the most impartial of weapons: it cuts both ways.

F.—And each way is peculiarly objectionable to your opponent.

S.—But for what am I indebted to you?

F.—For existence: the prevalence of me has made you possible.

S.—The benefit is not conspicuous; were it not for your quarrels, I should enjoy a quantity of elegant leisure.

F.—As a clodhopper.

S.—I should at least hop my clods in a humble and Christian spirit; and if some other fellow did did not so hop his—! I say no more.

F.—You have said enough; there would be war.

*   *   *   *   *

SOLDIER.—Why wear a cap and bells?

FOOL.—I hasten to crave pardon, and if spared will at once exchange them.

S.—For what?

F.—A helmet and feather.

S.—G "hang a calf-skin on those recreant limbs."

F.—'T is only wisdom should be bound in calf.

S.—Why?

F.—Because wisdom is the veal of which folly is the matured beef.

S.—Then folly should be garbed in cow-skin?

F.—Aye, that it might the more speedily appear for what it is—the naked truth.

S.—How should it?

F.—You would soon strip off its hide to make harness and trappings withal. No one thinks how much conquerors owe to cows.

*   *   *   *   *

FOOL.—Tell me, hero, what is strategy?

SOLDIER.—The art of laying two knives against one throat.

F.—And what are tactics?

S.—The art of driving them home.

F.—Supermundane lexicographer!

S.—I'll bust thy crust! (*Attempts to draw his sword, gets it between his legs, and falls along.*)

F. (*from a distance*)—Shall I summon an army, or a sexton? And will you have it of bronze, or marble?

* * * * *

FOOL.—When you have gained a great victory, how much of the glory goes to the horse whose back you bestrode?

SOLDIER.—Nonsense! A horse cannot appreciate glory; he prefers corn.

F.—And this you call non-appreciation! But listen. (*Reads*) "During the Crusades, a part of the armament of a Turkish ship was two hundred serpents." In the pursuit of glory you are at least not above employing humble auxiliaries. These be curious allies.

S.—What stuff a fool may talk! No true soldier would pit a serpent against a brave enemy. These worms were *sailors*.

F.—A nice distinction, truly! Did you ever, my most acute professor of vivisection, employ your trenchant blade in the splitting of hairs?

S.—I have split masses of them.

* * * * *

FOOL.—Speaking of the Crusades: at the siege of Acre, when a part of the wall had been thrown down by the Christians, the Pisans rushed into the breach, but the greater part of their army being at dinner, they were bloodily repulsed.

SOLDIER.—You appear to have a minute acquaintance with military history.

F.—Yes—being a fool. But was it not a sin and a shame that those feeders should not stir from their porridge to succour their suffering comrades?

S.—Pray why should a man neglect his business to oblige a friend?

F.—But they might have taken and sacked the city.

S.—The selfish gluttons!

*   *   *   *   *

SOLDIER.—Your presumption grows intolerable; I'll hold no further parley with thee.

FOOL.—"Herculean gentleman, I dread thy drubs; pity the lifted whites of both my eyes!"

S.—Then speak no more of the things you do but imperfectly understand.

F.—Such censorship would doom all tongues to silence. But show me wherein my knowledge is deficient.

S.—What is an *abattis*?

F.—Rubbish placed in front of a fort, to keep the rubbish outside from getting at the rubbish inside.

S.—Egad! I'll part thy hair!

DIVERS TALES

THE GRATEFUL BEAR

I hope all my little readers have heard the story of Mr.
Androcles and the lion; so I will relate it as nearly as I can
remember it, with the caution that Androcles must not be
confounded with the lion. If I had a picture representing
Androcles with a silk hat, and the lion with a knot in his tail,
the two might readily be distinguished; but the artist says he
won't make any such picture, and we must try to get on
without.

One day Androcles was gathering truffles in a forest, when he
found a lion's den; and, walking into it, he lay down and slept.
It was a custom, in his time, to sleep in lions' dens when
practicable. The lion was absent, inspecting a zoological
garden, and did not return until late; but he did return. He
was surprised to find a stranger in his menagerie without a
ticket; but, supposing him to be some contributor to a comic
paper, did not eat him: he was very well satisfied not to be
eaten by him. Presently Androcles awoke, wishing he had some
seltzer water, or something. (Seltzer water is good after a
night's debauch, and something—it is difficult to say what—is
good to begin the new debauch with). Seeing the lion eyeing
him, he began hastily to pencil his last will and testament upon
the rocky floor of the den. What was his surprise to see the lion
advance amicably and extend his right forefoot! Androcles,
however, was equal to the occasion: he met the friendly
overture with a cordial grasp of the hand, whereat the lion

howled—for he had a carpet-tack in his foot. Perceiving that he had made a little mistake, Androcles made such reparation as was in his power by pulling out the tack and putting it in his own foot.

After this the beast could not do too much for him. He went out every morning—carefully locking the door behind him—and returned every evening, bringing in a nice fat baby from an adjacent village, and laying it gratefully at his benefactor's feet. For the first few days something seemed to have gone wrong with the benefactor's appetite, but presently he took very kindly to the new diet; and, as he could not get away, he lodged there, rent-free, all the days of his life—which terminated very abruptly one evening when the lion had not met with his usual success in hunting.

All this has very little to do with my story: I throw it in as a classical allusion, to meet the demands of a literary fashion which has its origin in the generous eagerness of writers to give the public more than it pays for. But the story of Androcles was a favourite with the bear whose adventures I am about to relate.

One day this crafty brute carefully inserted a thorn between two of his toes, and limped awkwardly to the farm-house of Dame Pinworthy, a widow, who with two beautiful whelps infested the forest where he resided. He knocked at the open door, sent in his card, and was duly admitted to the presence of the lady, who inquired his purpose. By way of "defining his position" he held up his foot, and snuffled very dolorously. The lady adjusted her spectacles, took the paw in her lap (she, too, had heard the tale of Androcles), and, after a close scrutiny, discovered the thorn, which, as delicately as possible, she extracted, the patient making wry faces and howling dismally the while.

When it was all over, and she had assured him there was no charge, his gratitude was a passion to observe! He desired to embrace her at once; but this, although a widow of seven years' standing, she would by no means permit; she said she was not personally averse to hugging, "but what would her dear departed—boo-hoo!—say of it?" This was very absurd, for Mr. Boo-hoo had seven feet of solid earth above him, and it couldn't make much difference what he said, even supposing he had enough tongue left to say anything, which he had not. However, the polite beast respected her scruples; so the only way in which he could testify his gratitude was by remaining to dinner. They had the housedog for dinner that day, though, from some false notion of hospitable etiquette, the woman and children did not take any.

On the next day, punctually at the same hour, the bear came again with another thorn, and stayed to dinner as before. It was not much of a dinner this time—only the cat, and a roll of stair-carpet, with one or two pieces of sheet music; but true gratitude does not despise even the humblest means of expression. The succeeding day he came as before; but after being relieved of his torment, he found nothing prepared for him. But when he took to thoughtfully licking one of the little girl's hands, "that answered not with a caress," the mother thought better of it, and drove in a small heifer.

He now came every day; he was so old a friend that the formality of extracting the thorn was no longer observed; it would have contributed nothing to the good understanding that existed between him and the widow. He thought that three or four instances of Good Samaritanism afforded ample matter for perpetual gratitude. His constant visits were bad for the live stock of the farm; for some kind of beast had to be in readiness each day to furnish forth the usual feast, and this prevented multiplication. Most of the textile fabrics, too, had disappeared; for the appetite of this animal was at the same time cosmopolitan and exacting: it would accept almost anything in the way of *entremets*, but something it would have. A hearthrug, a hall-mat, a cushion, mattress, blanket, shawl, or other article of wearing apparel—anything, in short, that was easy of ingestion was graciously approved. The widow tried him once with a box of coals as dessert to some barn-yard fowls; but this he seemed to regard as a doubtful comestible, seductive to the palate, but obstinate in the stomach. A look at one of the children always brought him something else, no matter what he was then engaged on.

It was suggested to Mrs. Pinworthy that she should poison the bear; but, after trying about a hundredweight of strychnia, arsenic, and Prussic acid, without any effect other than what might be expected from mild tonics, she thought it would not be right to go into toxicology. So the poor Widow Pinworthy went on, patiently enduring the consumption of her cattle, sheep, and hogs, the evaporation of her poultry, and the taking off of her bed linen, until there were left only the clothing of herself and children, some curtains, a sickly lamb, and a pet pigeon. When the bear came for these she ventured to expostulate. In this she was perfectly successful: the animal permitted her to expostulate as long as she liked. Then he ate he lamb and pigeon, took in a dish-cloth or two, and went away just as contentedly as if she had not uttered a word.

Nothing edible now stood between her little daughters and the grave. Her mental agony was painful to her mind; she could scarcely have suffered more without an increase of unhappiness. She was roused to desperation; and next day, when she saw the bear leaping across the fields toward the house, she staggered from her seat and shut the door. It was singular what a difference it made; she always remembered it after that, and wished she had thought of it before.

*   *   *   *   *

Ambrose Bierce

THE SETTING SACHEM

'Twas an Injin chieftain, in feathers all fine,
Who stood on the ocean's rim;
There were numberless leagues of excellent brine—
But there wasn't enough for him.
So he knuckled a thumb in his painted eye,
And added a tear to the scant supply.

The surges were breaking with thund'rous voice,
The winds were a-shrieking shrill;
This warrior thought that a trifle of noise
Was needed to fill the bill.
So he lifted the top of his head off and scowled—
Exalted his voice, did this chieftain, and howled!

The sun was aflame in a field of gold
That hung o'er the Western Sea;
Bright banners of light were broadly unrolled,
As banners of light should be.
But no one was "speaking a piece" to that sun,
And therefore this Medicine Man begun:

"O much heap of bright! O big ball of warm!
I've tracked you from sea to sea!
For the Paleface has been at some pains to inform
Me, *you* are the emblem of *me*.
He says to me, cheerfully: 'Westward Ho!'
And westward I've hoed a most difficult row.

"Since you are the emblem of me, I presume
That I am the emblem of you,
And thus, as we're equals, 't is safe to assume,
That one great law governs us two.
So now if I set in the ocean with thee,
With thee I shall rise again out of the sea."

His eloquence first, and his logic the last!
Such orators die!—and he died:
The trump was against him—his luck bad—he "passed"—
And so he "passed out"—with the tide.
This Injin is rid of the world with a whim—
The world it is rid of his speeches and him.

FEODORA

Madame Yonsmit was a decayed gentlewoman who carried on her decomposition in a modest wayside cottage in Thuringia. She was an excellent sample of the Thuringian widow, a species not yet extinct, but trying very hard to become so. The same may be said of the whole genus. Madame Yonsmit was quite young, very comely, cultivated, gracious, and pleasing. Her home was a nest of domestic virtues, but she had a daughter who reflected but little credit upon the nest. Feodora was indeed a "bad egg"—a very wicked and ungrateful egg. You could see she was by her face. The girl had the most vicious countenance—it was repulsive! It was a face in which boldness struggled for the supremacy with cunning, and both were thrashed into subjection by avarice. It was this latter virtue in Feodora which kept her mother from having a taxable income.

Feodora's business was to beg on the highway. It wrung the heart of the honest amiable gentlewoman to have her daughter do this; but the h.a.g. having been reared in luxury, considered labour degrading—which it is—and there was not much to steal in that part of Thuringia. Feodora's mendicity would have provided an ample fund for their support, but unhappily that ingrate would hardly ever fetch home more than two or three shillings at a time. Goodness knows what she did with the rest.

Vainly the good woman pointed out the sin of coveteousness; vainly she would stand at the cottage door awaiting the child's return, and begin arguing the point with her the moment she came in sight: the receipts diminished daily until the average was less than tenpence—a sum upon which no born gentlewoman would deign to exist. So it became a matter of some importance to know where Feodora kept her banking account. Madame Yonsmit thought at first she would follow her and see; but although the good lady was as vigorous and sprightly as ever, carrying a crutch more for ornament than use, she abandoned this plan because it did not seem suitable to the dignity of a decayed gentlewoman. She employed a detective.

The foregoing particulars I have from Madame Yonsmit herself; for those immediately subjoining I am indebted to the detective, a skilful officer named Bowstr.

No sooner had the scraggy old hag communicated her suspicions than the officer knew exactly what to do. He first distributed hand-bills all over the country, stating that a certain person suspected of concealing money had better look sharp. He then went to the Home Secretary, and by not seeking to understate the real difficulties of the case, induced that functionary to offer a reward of a thousand pounds for the arrest of the malefactor. Next he proceeded to a distant town, and took into custody a clergyman who resembled Feodora in respect of wearing shoes. After these formal preliminaries he took up the case with some zeal. He was not at all actuated by a desire to obtain the reward, but by pure love of justice. The thought of securing the girl's private hoard for himself never for a moment entered his head.

He began to make frequent calls at the widow's cottage when Feodora was at home, when, by apparently careless conversation, he would endeavour to draw her out; but he was commonly frustrated by her old beast of a mother, who, when the girl's answers did not suit, would beat her unmercifully. So he took to meeting Feodora on the highway, and giving her coppers carefully marked. For months he kept this up with wonderful self-sacrifice—the girl being a mere uninteresting angel. He met her daily in the roads and forest. His patience

Ambrose Bierce

never wearied, his vigilance never flagged. Her most careless glances were conscientiously noted, her lightest words treasured up in his memory. Meanwhile (the clergyman having been unjustly acquitted) he arrested everybody he could get his hands on. Matters went on in this way until it was time for the grand *coup*.

The succeeding-particulars I have from the lips of Feodora herself.

When that horrid Bowstr first came to the house Feodora thought he was rather impudent, but said, little about it to her mother—not desiring to have her back broken. She merely avoided him as much as she dared, he was so frightfully ugly. But she managed to endure him until he took to waylaying her on the highway, hanging about her all day, interfering with the customers, and walking home with her at night. Then her dislike deepened into disgust; and but for apprehensions not wholly unconnected with a certain crutch, she would have sent him about his business in short order. More than a thousand million times she told him to be off and leave her alone, but men are such fools—particularly this one.

What made Bowstr exceptionally disagreeable was his shameless habit of making fun of Feodora's mother, whom he declared crazy as a loon. But the maiden bore everything as well as she could, until one day the nasty thing put his arm about her waist and kissed her before her very face; *then* she felt—well, it is not clear how she felt, but of one thing she was quite sure: after having such a shame put upon her by this insolent brute, she would never go back under her dear mother's roof—never. She was too proud for *that*, at any rate. So she ran away with Mr. Bowstr, and married him.

The conclusion of this history I learned for myself.

Upon hearing of her daughter's desertion Madame Yonsmit went clean daft. She vowed she could bear betrayal, could endure decay, could stand being a widow, would not repine at being left alone in her old age (whenever she should become old), and could patiently submit to the sharper than a serpent's thanks of having a toothless child generally. But to be a mother-in-law! No, no; that was a plane of degradation to which she positively would *not* descend. So she employed me to cut her throat. It was the toughest throat I ever cut in all my life.

Ambrose Bierce

THE LEGEND OF IMMORTAL TRUTH

A bear, having spread him a notable feast,
Invited a famishing fox to the place.
"I've killed me," quoth he, "an edible beast
As ever distended the girdle of priest
With 'spread of religion,' or 'inward grace.'
To my den I conveyed her,
I bled her and flayed her,
I hung up her skin to dry;
Then laid her naked, to keep her cool,
On a slab of ice from the frozen pool;
And there we will eat her—you and I."

The fox accepts, and away they walk,
Beguiling the time with courteous talk.
You'd ne'er have suspected, to see them smile,
The bear was thinking, the blessed while,
How, when his guest should be off his guard,
With feasting hard,
He'd give him a "wipe" that would spoil his style.
You'd never have thought, to see them bow,
The fox was reflecting deeply how
He would best proceed, to circumvent
His host, and prig
The entire pig—
Or other bird to the same intent.
When Strength and Cunning in love combine,
Be sure 't is to more than merely dine.

The while these biters ply the lip,
A mile ahead the muse shall skip:
The poet's purpose she best may serve
Inside the den—if she have the nerve.
Behold! laid out in dark recess,
A ghastly goat in stark undress,
Pallid and still on her gelid bed,
And indisputably very dead.
Her skin depends from a couple of pins—
And here the most singular statement begins;
For all at once the butchered beast,
With easy grace for one deceased,
Upreared her head,
Looked round, and said,
Very distinctly for one so dead:
"The nights are sharp, and the sheets are thin:
I find it uncommonly cold herein!"

I answer not how this was wrought:
All miracles surpass my thought.
They're vexing, say you? and dementing?
Peace, peace! they're none of my inventing.
But lest too much of mystery
Embarrass this true history,
I'll not relate how that this goat
Stood up and stamped her feet, to inform'em
With—what's the word?—I mean, to warm'em;
Nor how she plucked her rough *capote*
From off the pegs where Bruin threw it,
And o'er her quaking body drew it;
Nor how each act could so befall:
I'll only swear she did them all;
Then lingered pensive in the grot,
As if she something had forgot,
Till a humble voice and a voice of pride
Were heard, in murmurs of love, outside.
Then, like a rocket set aflight,
She sprang, and streaked it for the light!

Ambrose Bierce

Ten million million years and a day
Have rolled, since these events, away;
But still the peasant at fall of night,
Belated therenear, is oft affright
By sounds of a phantom bear in flight;
A breaking of branches under the hill;
The noise of a going when all is still!
And hens asleep on the perch, they say,
Cackle sometimes in a startled way,
As if they were dreaming a dream that mocks
The lope and whiz of a fleeting fox!

Half we're taught, and teach to youth,
And praise by rote,
Is not, but merely stands for, truth.
So of my goat:
She's merely designed to represent
The truth—"immortal" to this extent:
Dead she may be, and skinned—*frappe*—
Hid in a dreadful den away;
Prey to the Churches—(any will do,
Except the Church of me and you.)
The simplest miracle, even then,
Will get her up and about again.

CONVERTING A PRODIGAL

Little Johnny was a saving youth—one who from early infancy had cultivated a provident habit. When other little boys were wasting their substance in riotous gingerbread and molasses candy, investing in missionary enterprises which paid no dividends, subscribing to the North Labrador Orphan Fund, and sending capital out of the country gene rally, Johnny would be sticking sixpences into the chimney-pot of a big tin house with "BANK" painted on it in red letters above an illusory door. Or he would put out odd pennies at appalling rates of interest, with his parents, and bank the income. He was never weary of dropping coppers into that insatiable chimney-pot, and leaving them there. In this latter respect he differed notably from his elder brother, Charlie; for, although Charles was fond of banking too, he was addicted to such frequent runs upon the institution with a hatchet, that it kept his parents honourably poor to purchase banks for him; so they were reluctantly compelled to discourage the depositing element in his panicky nature.

Johnny was not above work, either; to him "the dignity of labour" was not a juiceless platitude, as it is to me, but a living, nourishing truth, as satisfying and wholesome as that two sides of a triangle are equal to one side of bacon. He would hold horses for gentlemen who desired to step into a bar to inquire for letters. He would pursue the fleeting pig at the behest of a drover. He would carry water to the lions of a travelling menagerie, or do anything, for gain. He was sharp-witted too: before conveying a drop of comfort to the parching king of beasts, he would stipulate for six-pence instead of the usual free ticket—or "tasting order," so to speak. He cared not a button for the show.

The first hard work Johnny did of a morning was to look over the house for fugitive pins, needles, hair-pins, matches, and other unconsidered trifles; and if he sometimes found these where nobody had lost them, he made such reparation as was in his power by losing them again where nobody but he could find them. In the course of time, when he had garnered a good many, he would "realize," and bank the proceeds.

Nor was he weakly superstitious, this Johnny. You could not fool *him* with the Santa Claus hoax on Christmas Eve: he would lie awake all night, as sceptical as a priest; and along toward morning, getting quietly out of bed, would examine the pendent stockings of the other children, to satisfy himself the predicted presents were not there; and in the morning it always turned out that they were not. Then, when the other children cried because they did not get anything, and the parents affected surprise (as if they really believed in the venerable fiction), Johnny was too manly to utter a whimper: he would simply slip out of the back door, and engage in traffic with affluent orphans; disposing of woolly horses, tin whistles, marbles, tops, dolls, and sugar archangels, at a ruinous discount for cash. He continued these provident courses for nine long years, always banking his accretions with scrupulous care. Everybody predicted he would one day be a merchant prince or a railway king; and some added he would sell his crown to the junk-dealers.

His unthrifty brother, meanwhile, kept growing worse and worse. He was so careless of wealth—so so wastefully extravagant of lucre—that Johnny felt it his duty at times to clandestinely assume control of the fraternal finances, lest the habit of squandering should wreck the fraternal moral sense. It was plain that Charles had entered upon the broad road which leads from the cradle to the workhouse—and that he rather liked the travelling. So profuse was his prodigality that there were grave suspicions as to his method of acquiring what he so openly disbursed. There was but one opinion as to the melancholy termination of his career—a termination which he seemed to regard as eminently desirable. But one day, when the good pastor put it at him in so many words, Charles gave token of some apprehension.

"Do you really think so, sir?" said he, thoughtfully; "ain't you playin' it on me?"

"I assure you, Charles," said the good man, catching a ray of hope from the boy's dawning seriousness, "you will certainly end your days in a workhouse, unless you speedily abandon your course of extravagance. There is nothing like habit—nothing!"

Charles may have thought that, considering his frequent and lavish contributions to the missionary fund, the parson was rather hard upon him; but he did not say so. He went away in mournful silence, and began pelting a blind beggar with coppers.

One day, when Johnny had been more than usually provident, and Charles proportionately prodigal, their father, having exhausted moral suasion to no apparent purpose, determined to have recourse to a lower order of argument: he would try to win Charles to economy by an appeal to his grosser nature. So he convened the entire family, and,

"Johnny," said he, "do you think you have much money in your bank? You ought to have saved a considerable sum in nine years."

Johnny took the alarm in a minute: perhaps there was some barefooted little girl to be endowed with Sunday-school books.

"No," he answered, reflectively, "I don't think there can be much. There's been a good deal of cold weather this winter, and you know how metal shrinks! No-o-o, I'm sure there can't be only a little."

"Well, Johnny, you go up and bring down your bank. We'll see. Perhaps Charles may be right, after all; and it's not worth while to save money. I don't want a son of mine to get into a bad habit unless it pays."

So Johnny travelled reluctantly up to his garret, and went to the corner where his big tin bank-box had sat on a chest undisturbed for years. He had long ago fortified himself against temptation by vowing never to even shake it; for he remembered that formerly when Charles used to shake his, and rattle the coins inside, he always ended by smashing in the roof. Johnny approached his bank, and taking hold of the cornice on either side, braced himself, gave a strong lift upwards, and keeled over upon his back with the edifice atop of him, like one of the figures in a picture of the great Lisbon earthquake! There was but a single coin in it; and that, by an ingenious device, was suspended in the centre, so that every piece popped in at the chimney would clink upon it in passing through Charlie's little hole into Charlie's little stocking hanging innocently beneath.

Of course restitution was out of the question; and even Johnny felt that any merely temporal punishment would be weakly inadequate to the demands of justice. But that night, in the dead silence of his chamber, Johnny registered a great and solemn swear that so soon as he could worry together a little capital, he would fling his feeble remaining energies into the spendthrift business. And he did so.

FOUR JACKS AND A KNAVE

In the "backwoods" of Pennsylvania stood a little mill. The miller appertaining unto this mill was a Pennsylvania Dutchman—a species of animal in which for some centuries *sauerkraut* has been usurping the place of sense. In Hans Donnerspiel the usurpation was not complete; he still knew enough to go in when it rained, but he did not know enough to stay there after the storm had blown over. Hans was known to a large circle of friends and admirers as about the worst miller in those parts; but as he was the only one, people who quarrelled with an exclusively meat diet continued to patronize him. He was honest, as all stupid people are; but he was careless. So absent-minded was he, that sometimes when grinding somebody's wheat he would thoughtlessly turn into the "hopper" a bag of rye, a lot of old beer-bottles, or a basket of fish. This made the flour so peculiar, that the people about there never knew what it was to be well a day in all their lives. There were so many local diseases in that vicinity, that a doctor from twenty miles away could not have killed a patient in a week.

Hans meant well; but he had a hobby—a hobby that he did not ride: that does not express it: it rode him. It spurred him so hard, that the poor wretch could not pause a minute to see what he was putting into his mill. This hobby was the purchase of jackasses. He expended all his income in this diversion, and his mill was fairly sinking under its weight of mortgages. He had more jackasses than he had hairs on his head, and, as a rule, they were thinner. He was no mere

Ambrose Bierce

amateur collector either, but a sharp discriminating *connoisseur*. He would buy a fat globular donkey if he could not do better; but a lank shabby one was the apple of his eye. He rolled such a one, as it were, like a sweet morsel under his tongue.

Hans's nearest neighbour was a worthless young scamp named Jo Garvey, who lived mainly by hunting and fishing. Jo was a sharp-witted rascal, without a single scruple between, himself and fortune. With a tithe of Hans's industry he might have been almost anything; but his dense laziness always rose up like a stone wall about him, shutting him in like a toad in a rock. The exact opposite of Hans in almost every respect, he was notably similar in one: he had a hobby. Jo's hobby was the selling of jackasses.

One day, while Hans's upper and nether mill-stones were making it lively for a mingled grist of corn, potatoes, and young chickens, he heard Joseph calling outside. Stepping to the door, he saw him holding three halters to which were appended three donkeys.

"I say, Hans," said he, "here are three fine animals for your stud. I have brought 'em up from the egg, and I know 'em to be first-class. But they 're not so big as I expected, and you may have 'em for a sack of oats each."

Hans was delighted. He had not the least doubt in the world that Joe had stolen them; but it was a fixed principle with him never to let a donkey go away and say he was a hard man to deal with. He at once brought out and delivered the oats. Jo gravely examined the quality, and placing a sack across each animal, calmly led them away.

When he had gone, it occurred to Hans that he had less oats and no more asses than he had before.

"Tuyfel!" he exclaimed, scratching his pow; "I puy dot yackasses, und I don't vos god 'im so mooch as I didn't haf 'im before—ain't it?"

Very much to his comfort it was, therefore, to see Jo come by next day leading the same animals.

"Hi!" he shrieked; "you prings me to my yackasses. You gif me to my broberdy back!"

"Oh, very well, Hans. If you want to crawfish out of a fair bargain, all right. I'll give you back your donkeys, and you give me back my oats."

"Yaw, yaw," assented the mollified miller; "you his von honest shentlemans as I vos efer vent anyvhere. But I don't god ony more oats, und you moost dake vheat, eh?"

And fetching out three sacks of wheat, he handed them over. Jo was proceeding to lay these upon the backs of the animals; but this was too thin for even Hans.

"Ach! you tief-veller! you leabs dis yackasses in me, und go right avay off; odther I bust your het mid a gloob, don't it?"

So Joseph was reluctantly constrained to hang the donkeys to a fence. While he did this, Hans was making a desperate attempt to think. Presently he brightened up:

"Yo, how you coom by dot vheat all de dime?"

"Why, old mudhead, you gave it to me for the jacks."

"Und how you coom by dot oats pooty soon avhile ago?"

"Why, I gave that to you for them," said Joseph, pressed very hard for a reply.

"Vell, den, you goes vetch me back to dot oats so gwicker as a lamb gedwinkle his dail—hay?"

"All right, Hans. Lend me the donkeys to carry off my wheat, and I 'll bring back your oats on 'em."

Joseph was beginning to despair; but no objection being made, he loaded up the grain, and made off with his docile caravan. In a half-hour he returned with the donkeys, but of course without anything else.

"I zay, Yo, where is dis oats I hear zo mooch dalk aboud still?"

"Oh, curse you and your oats!" growled Jo, with simulated anger. "You make such a fuss about a bargain, I have decided not to trade. Take your old donkeys, and call it square!"

"Den vhere mine vheat is?"

"Now look here, Hans; that wheat is yours, is it?"

"Yaw, yaw."

"And the donkeys are yours, eh?"

"Yaw, yaw."

"And the wheat's been yours all the time, has it?"

"Yaw, yaw."

"Well, so have the donkeys. I took 'em out of your pasture in the first place. Now what have you got to complain of?"

The Dutchman reflected all over his head with' his forefinger-nail.

"Gomblain? I no gomblain ven it is all right. I zee now I vos made a mistaken. Coom, dake a drinks."

Jo left the animals standing, and went inside, where they pledged one another in brimming mugs of beer. Then taking

Hans by the hand,

"I am sorry," said he, "we can't trade. Perhaps some other day you will be more reasonable. Good bye!"

And Joseph departed leading away the donkeys!

Hans stood for some moments gazing after him with a complacent smile making his fat face ridiculous. Then turning to his mill-stones, he shook his head with an air of intense self-satisfaction:

"Py donner! Dot Yo Garfey bees a geen, shmard yockey, but he gonnot spiel me svoppin' yackasses!"

DR. DEADWOOD, I PRESUME

My name is Shandy, and this is the record of my Sentimental Journey. Mr. Ames Jordan Gannett, proprietor's son of the "York—," with which paper I am connected by marriage, sent me a post-card in a sealed envelope, asking me to call at a well-known restaurant in Regent Street. I was then at a well-known restaurant in Houndsditch. I put on my worst and only hat, and went. I found Mr. Gannett, at dinner, eating pease with his knife, in the manner of his countrymen. He opened the conversation, characteristically, thus:

"Where's Dr. Deadwood?"

After several ineffectual guesses I had a happy thought. I asked him:

"Am I my brother's bar-keeper?"

Mr. Gannett pondered deeply, with his forefinger alongside his nose. Finally he replied:

"I give it up."

He continued to eat for some moments in profound silence, as that of a man very much in earnest. Suddenly he resumed:

"Here is a blank cheque, signed. I will send you all my father's personal property to-morrow. Take this and find Dr. Deadwood. Find him actually if you can, but find him. Away!"

I did as requested; that is, I took the cheque. Having supplied myself with such luxuries as were absolutely necessary, I retired to my lodgings. Upon my table in the centre of the room were spread some clean white sheets of foolscap, and sat a bottle of black ink. It was a good omen: the virgin paper was typical of the unexplored interior of Africa; the sable ink represented the night of barbarism, or the hue of barbarians, indifferently.

Now began the most arduous undertaking mentioned in the "York—," I mean in history. Lighting my pipe, and fixing my eye upon the ink and paper, I put my hands behind my back and took my departure from the hearthrug toward the Interior. Language fails me; I throw myself upon the reader's imagination. Before I had taken two steps, my vision alighted upon the circular of a quack physician, which I had brought home the day before around a bottle of hair-wash. I now saw the words, "Twenty-one fevers!" This prostrated me for I know not how long. Recovering, I took a step forward, when my eyes fastened themselves upon my pen-wiper, worked into the similitude of a tiger. This compelled me to retreat to the hearthrug for reinforcements. The red-and-white dog displayed upon that article turned a deaf ear to my entreaties; nothing would move him.

A torrent of rain now began falling outside, and I knew the roads were impassable; but, chafing with impatience, I resolved upon another advance. Cautiously proceeding *via* the sofa, my attention fell upon a scrap of newspaper; and, to my unspeakable disappointment, I read:

"The various tribes of the Interior are engaged in a bitter warfare."

It may have related to America, but I could not afford to hazard all upon a guess. I made a wide *detour* by way of the coal-scuttle, and skirted painfully along the sideboard. All this consumed so much time that my pipe expired in gloom, and I went back to the hearthrug to get a match off the chimney-piece. Having done so, I stepped over to the table and sat down, taking up the pen and spreading the paper between myself and the ink-bottle. It was late, and something must be done. Writing the familiar word Ujijijijijiji, I caught a neighbourly cockroach, skewered him upon a pin, and fastened him in the centre of the word. At this supreme moment I felt inclined to fall upon his neck and devour him with kisses; but knowing by experience that cockroaches are not good to eat, I restrained my feelings. Lifting my hat, I said:

"Dr. Deadwood, I presume?"

He did not deny it!

Seeing he was feeling sick, I gave him a bit of cheese and cheered him up a trifle. After he was well restored,

"Tell me," said I, "is it true that the Regent's Canal falls into Lake Michigan, thence running uphill to Omaha, as related by Ptolemy, thence spirally to Melbourne, where it joins the delta of the Ganges and becomes an affluent of the Albert Nicaragua, as Herodotus maintains?"

HE DID NOT DENY IT!

The rest is known to the public.

NUT-CRACKING

In the city of Algammon resided the Prince Champou, who was madly enamoured of the Lady Capilla. She returned his affection—unopened.

In the matter of back-hair the Lady Capilla was blessed even beyond her deserts. Her natural pigtail was so intolerably long that she employed two pages to look after it when she walked out; the one a few yards behind her, the other at the extreme end of the line. Their names were Dan and Beersheba, respectively.

Aside from salaries to these dependents, and quite apart from the consideration of macassar, the possession of all this animal filament was financially unprofitable: the hair market was buoyant, and hers represented a large amount of idle capital. And it was otherwise a source of annoyance and irritation; for all the young men of the city were hotly in love with her, and skirmishing for a love-lock. They seldom troubled Dan much, but the outlying Beersheba had an animated time of it. He was subject to constant incursions, and was always in a riot.

The picture I have drawn to illustrate this history shows nothing of all these squabbles. My pen revels in the battle's din, but my peaceful pencil loves to depict the scenes I know something about.

Although the Lady Capilla was unwilling to reciprocate the passion of Champou the man, she was not averse to quiet interviews with Champou the Prince. In the course of one of these (see my picture), as she sat listening to his carefully-rehearsed and really artistic avowals, with her tail hanging out of the window, she suddenly interrupted him:

"My dear Prince," said she, "it is all nonsense, you know, to ask for my heart; but I am not mean; you shall have a lock of my hair."

"Do you think," replied the Prince, "that I could be so sordid as to accept a single jewel from that glorious crown? I love this hair of yours very dearly, I admit, but only because of its connection with your divine head. Sever that connection, and I should value it no more than I would a tail plucked from its native cow."

This comparison seems to me a very fine one, but tastes differ, and to the Lady Capilla it seemed quite the reverse. Rising indignantly, she marched away, her queue running in through the window and gradually tapering off the interview, as it were. Prince Champou saw that he had missed his opportunity, and resolved to repair his error. Straightway he forged an order on Beersheba for thirty yards of love-lock. To serve this writ he sent his business partner; for the Prince was wont to beguile his dragging leisure by tonsorial diversions in an obscure quarter of the town. At first Beersheba was sceptical, but when he saw the writing in real ink, his scruples vanished, and he chopped off the amount of souvenir demanded.

Now Champou's partner was the Court barber, and by the use of a peculiar hair oil which the two of them had concocted, they soon managed to balden the pates of all the male aristocracy of the place. Then, to supply the demand so created, they devised beautiful wigs from the Lady Capilla's lost tresses, which they sold at a marvellous profit. And so they were enabled to retire from this narrative with good incomes.

It was known that the Lady Capilla, who, since the alleged murder of one Beersheba, had shut herself up like a hermit, or a jack-knife, would re-enter society; and a great ball was given to do her honour. The feauty, bank, and rashion of Algammon had assembled in the Guildhall for that purpose. While the revelry was at its fiercest, the dancing at its loosest, the rooms at their hottest, and the perspiration at spring-tide, there was a sound of wheels outside, begetting an instant hush of expectation within. The dancers ceased to spin, and all the gentlemen crowded about the door. As the Lady Capilla entered, these instinctively fell into two lines, and she passed down the space between, with her little tail behind her. As the end of the latter came into the room, the wigs of the two gentlemen nearest the door leaped off to join their parent stem. In their haste to recover them the two gentlemen bent eagerly forward, knocking their shining pows together with a vehemence that shattered them like egg-shells. The wigs of the next pair were similarly affected; and in seeking to recover them the pair similarly perished. Then, *crack! spat! pash!*—at every step the lady took there were two heads that beat as one. In three minutes there was but a single living male in the room. He was an odd one, who, having a lady opposite him, had merely pitched himself headlong into her stomach, doubling her like a lemon-squeezer.

It was merry to see the Lady Capilla floating through the mazy dance that night, with all those wigs fighting for their old places in her pigtail.

Ambrose Bierce

THE MAGICIAN'S LITTLE JOKE

About the middle of the fifteenth century there dwelt in the Black Forest a pretty but unfashionable young maiden named Simprella Whiskiblote. The first of these names was hers in monopoly; the other she enjoyed in common with her father. Simprella was the most beautiful fifteenth-century girl I ever saw. She had coloured eyes, a complexion, some hair, and two lips very nearly alike, which partially covered a lot of teeth. She was gifted with the complement of legs commonly worn at that period, supporting a body to which were loosely attached, in the manner of her country, as many arms as she had any use for, inasmuch as she was not required to hold baby. But all these charms were only so many objective points for the operations of the paternal cudgel; for this father of hers was a hard, unfeeling man, who had no bowels of compassion for his bludgeon. He would put it to work early, and keep it going all day; and when it was worn out with hard service, instead of rewarding it with steady employment, he would cruelly throw it aside and get a fresh one. It is scarcely to be wondered at that a girl harried in this way should be driven to the insane expedient of falling in love.

Near the neat mud cottage in which Simprella vegetated was a dense wood, extending for miles in various directions, according to the point from which it was viewed. By a method readily understood, it had been so arranged that it was the next easiest thing in the world to get into it, and the very easiest thing in the world to stay there.

In the centre of this labyrinth was a castle of the early promiscuous order of architecture—an order which was until recently much employed in the construction of powder-works, but is now entirely exploded. In this baronial hall lived an eligible single party—a giant so tall he used a step-ladder to put on his hat, and could not put his hands into his pockets without kneeling. He lived entirely alone, and gave himself up to the practice of iniquity, devising prohibitory liquor laws, imposing the income tax, and drinking shilling claret. But, seeing Simprella one day, he bent himself into the form of a horse-shoe magnet to look into her eyes. Whether it was his magnetic attitude acting upon a young heart steeled by adversity, or his chivalric forbearance in not eating her, I know not: I only know that from that moment she became riotously enamoured of him; and the reader may accept either the scientific or the popular explanation, according to the bent of his mind.

She at once asked the giant in marriage, and obtained the consent of his parents by betraying her father into their hands; explaining to them, however, that he was not good to eat, but might be drunk on the premises.

The marriage proved a very happy one, but the household duties of the bride were extremely irksome. It fatigued her to dress the beeves for dinner; it nearly broke her back to black her lord's boots without any scaffolding. It took her all day to perform any kindly little office for him. But she bore it all uncomplainingly, until one morning he asked her to part his back hair; then the bent sapling of her spirit flew up and hit him in the face. She gathered up some French novels, and retired to a lonely tower to breathe out her soul in unavailing regrets.

One day she saw below her in the forest a dear gazelle, gladding her with its soft black eye. She leaned out of the window, and said *Scat!* The animal did not move. Then she waved her arms—above described—and said *Shew!* This time he did not move as much as he did before. Simprella decided he must have a bill against her; so she closed her shutters, drew down the blind, and pinned the curtains together. A moment later she opened them and peeped out. Then she went down to examine his collar, that she might order one like it.

When the gazelle saw Simprella approach, he arose, and, beckoning with his tail, made off slowly into the wood. Then Simprella perceived this was a supernatural gazelle—a variety now extinct, but which then pervaded the Schwarzwald in considerable quantity—sent by some good magician, who owed the giant a grudge, to pilot her out of the forest. Nothing could exceed her joy at this discovery: she whistled a dirge, sang a Latin hymn, and preached a funeral discourse all in one breath. Such were the artless methods by which the full heart in the fifteenth century was compelled to express its gratitude for benefits; the advertising columns of the daily papers were not then open to the benefactor's pen.

All would now have been well, but for the fact that it was not. In following her deliverer, Simprella observed that his golden collar was inscribed with the mystic words—HANDS OFF! She tried hard to obey the injunction; she did her level best; she—but why amplify? Simprella was a woman.

No sooner had her fingers touched the slender chain depending from the magic collar, than the poor animal's eyes emitted twin tears, which coursed silently but firmly down his nose, vacating it more in sorrow than in anger. Then he looked up reproachfully into her face. Those were his first tears—this was his last look. In two minutes by the watch he was blind as a mole!

There is but little more to tell. The giant ate himself to death; the castle mouldered and crumbled into pig-pens; empires rose and fell; kings ascended their thrones, and got down again; mountains grew grey, and rivers bald-headed; suits in chancery were brought and decided, and those from the tailor were paid for; the ages came, like maiden aunts, uninvited, and lingered till they became a bore—and still Simprella, with the magician's curse upon her, conducted her sightless guide through the interminable wilderness!

To all others the labyrinth had yielded up its clue. The hunter threaded its maze; the woodman plunged confidently into its innermost depths; the peasant child gathered ferns unscared in its sunless dells. But often the child abandoned his botany in terror, the woodman bolted for home, and the hunter's heart went down into his boots, at the sight of a fair young spectre leading a blind phantom through the silent glades. I saw them there in 1860, while I was gunning. I shot them.

SEAFARING

My envious rivals have always sought to cast discredit upon the following tale, by affirming that mere unadorned truth does not constitute a work of literary merit. Be it so: I care not what they call it. A rose with any other smell would be as sweet.

In the autumn of 1868 I wanted to go from Sacramento, California, to San Francisco. I at once went to the railway office and bought a ticket, the clerk telling me that would take me there. But when I tried it, it wouldn't. Vainly I laid it on the railway and sat down upon it: it would not move; and every few minutes an engine would come along and crowd me off the track. I never travelled by so badly managed a line!

I then resolved to go by way of the river, and took passage on a steamboat. The engineer of this boat had once been a candidate for the State Legislature while I was editing a newspaper. Stung to madness by the arguments I had advanced against his election (which consisted mainly in relating how that his cousin was hanged for horse-stealing, and how that his sister had an intolerable squint which a free people could never abide), he had sworn to be revenged. After his defeat I had confessed the charges were false, so far as he personally was concerned, but this did not seem to appease him. He declared he would "get even on me," and he did: he blew up the boat.

Being thus summarily set ashore, I determined that I would be independent of common carriers destitute of common courtesy. I purchased a wooden box, just large enough to admit one, and not transferable. I lay down in this, double-locked it on the outside, and carrying it to the river, launched it upon the watery waste. The box, I soon discovered, had an hereditary tendency to turn over. I had parted my hair in the middle before embarking, but the precaution was inadequate; it secured not immunity, only impartiality, the box turning over one way as readily as the other. I could counteract this evil only by shifting my tobacco from cheek to cheek, and in this way I got on tolerably well until my navy sprang a leak near the stern.

I now began to wish I had not locked down the cover; I could have got out and walked ashore. But it was childish to give way to foolish regrets; so I lay perfectly quiet, and yelled. Presently I thought of my jack-knife. By this time the ship was so water-logged as to be a little more stable. This enabled me to get the knife from my pocket without upsetting more than six or eight times, and inspired hope. Taking the whittle between my teeth, I turned over upon my stomach, and cut a hole through the bottom near the bow. Turning back again, I awaited the result. Most men would have awaited the result, I think, if they could not have got out. For some time there was no result. The ship was too deeply laden astern, where my feet were, and water will not run up hill unless it is paid to do it. But when I called in all my faculties for a good earnest think, the weight of my intellect turned the scale. It was like a cargo of pig-lead in the forecastle. The water, which for nearly an hour I had kept down by drinking it as it rose about my lips, began to run out at the hole I had scuttled, faster than it could be admitted at the one in the stern; and in a few moments the bottom was so dry you might have lighted a match upon it, if you had been there, and obtained the captain's permission.

I was all right now. I had got into San Pablo Bay, where it was all plain sailing. If I could manage to keep off the horizon I should be somewhere before daylight. But a new annoyance was in store for me. The steamboats on these waters are constructed of very frail materials, and whenever one came into collision with my flotilla, she immediately sank. This was most exasperating, for the piercing shrieks of the hapless crews and passengers prevented my getting any sleep. Such disagreeable voices as these people had would have tortured an ear of corn. I felt as if I would like to step out and beat them soft-headed with a club; though of course I had not the heart to do so while the padlock held fast.

The reader, if he is obliging, will remember that there was formerly an obstruction in the harbour of San Francisco, called Blossom Rock, which was some fathoms under water, but not fathoms enough to suit shipmasters. It was removed by an engineer named Von Schmidt. This person bored a hole in it, and sent down some men who gnawed out the whole interior, leaving the rock a mere shell. Into this drawing-room suite were inserted thirty tons of powder, ten barrels of nitro-glycerine, and a woman's temper. Von Schmidt then put in something explosive, and corked up the opening, leaving a long wire hanging out. When all these preparations were complete, the inhabitants of San Francisco came out to see the fun. They perched thickly upon Telegraph Hill from base to summit; they swarmed innumerable upon the beach; the whole region was black with them. All that day they waited, and came again the next. Again they were disappointed, and again they returned full of hope. For three long weeks they did nothing but squat upon that eminence, looking fixedly at the wrong place. But when it transpired that Von Schmidt had hastily left the State directly he had completed his preparations, leaving the wire floating in the water, in the hope that some electrical eel might swim against it and ignite the explosives, the people began to abate their ardour, and move out of town. They said it might be a good while before a qualified gymnotus would pass that way, although the State Ichthyologer assured them that he had put some eels' eggs into the head waters of the Sacramento River not two weeks previously. But the country was very beautiful at that time of the year, and the people would not wait. So when the explosion really occurred, there wasn't anybody in the vicinity to witness it. It was a stupendous explosion all the same, as the unhappy gymnotus discovered to his cost.

Now, I have often thought that if this mighty convulsion had occurred a year or two earlier than it really did, it would have been bad for me as I floated idly past, unconscious of danger. As it was, my little bark was carried out into the broad Pacific, and sank in ten thousand fathoms of the coldest water!—it makes my teeth chatter to relate it!

TONY ROLLO'S CONCLUSION

To a degree unprecedented in the Rollo family, of Illinois, Antony was an undutiful son. He was so undutiful that he may be said to have been preposterous. There were seven other sons—Antony was the eldest. His younger brothers were a nice, well-behaved bevy of boys as ever you saw. They always attended Sunday School regularly; arriving just before the Doxology (I think Sunday School exercises terminate that way), and sitting in a solemn row on a fence outside, waiting with pious patience for the girls to come forth; then they walked home with them as far as their respective gates. They were an obedient seven, too; they knew well enough the respect due to paternal authority, and when their father told them what was what, and which side up it ought to lie, they never tarried until he had more than picked up a hickory cudgel before tacitly admitting the correctness of the riper judgment. Had the old gentleman commanded the digging of seven graves, and the fabrication of seven board coffins to match, these necessaries would have been provided with unquestioning alacrity.

But Antony, I bleed to state, was of an impractical, pensive turn. He despised industry, scoffed at Sunday-schooling, set up a private standard of morals, and rebelled against natural authority. He wouldn't be a dutiful son—not for money! He had no natural affections, and loved nothing so well as to sit and think. He was tolerably thoughtful all the time; but with some farming implement in his hand he came out strong. He has been known to take an axe between his knees, and sit on a stump in a "clearing" all day, wrapt in a single continuous meditation. And when interrupted by the interposition of night, or by the superposition of the paternal hickory, he would resume the meditation, next day, precisely where he left off, going on, and on, and on, in one profound and inscrutable think. It was a common remark in the neighbourhood that "If Tony Rollo didn't let up, he'd think his ridiculous white head off!" And on divers occasions when the old man's hickory had fallen upon that fleecy globe with unusual ardour, Tony really did think it off—until the continued pain convinced him it was there yet.

You would like to know what Tony was thinking of, all these years. That is what they all wanted to know; but he didn't seem to tell. When the subject was mentioned he would always try to get away; and if he could not avoid a direct question, he would blush and stammer in so distressing a confusion that the doctor forbade all allusion to the matter, lest the young man should have a convulsion. It was clear enough, however, that the subject of Tony's meditation was "more than average interes*t*in'," as his father phrased it; for sometimes he would give it so grave consideration that observers would double their anxiety about the safety of his head, which he seemed in danger of snapping off with solemn nods; and at other times he would laugh immoderately, smiting his thigh or holding his sides in uncontrollable merriment. But it went on without abatement, and without any disclosure; went on until his poor mother's curiosity had worried her grey hairs in sorrow to the grave; went on until his father, having worn out all the hickory saplings on the place, had made a fair beginning upon the young oaks; went on until all the seven brothers, having married a Sunday-school girl each, had erected comfortable log-houses upon outlying corners of the father-in-legal farms; on, and ever on, until Tony was forty years of age! This appeared to be a turning-point in Tony's career—at this time a subtle change stole into his life, affecting both his inner and his outer self: he worked less than formerly, and thought a good deal more!

Ambrose Bierce

Years afterwards, when the fraternal seven were well-to-do freeholders, with clouds of progeny, making their hearts light and their expenses heavy—when the old homestead was upgrown with rank brambles, and the live-stock long extinct—when the aged father had so fallen into the sere and yellow leaf that he couldn't hit hard enough to hurt—Tony, the mere shadow of his former self, sat, one evening, in the chimney corner, thinking very hard indeed. His father and three or four skeleton hounds were the only other persons present; the old gentleman quietly shelling a peck of Indian corn given by a grateful neighbour whose cow he had once pulled out of the mire, and the hounds thinking how cheerfully they would have assisted him had Nature kindly made them graminivorous. Suddenly Tony spake.

"Father," said he, looking straight across the top of the axe-handle which he held between his knees as a mental stimulant, "father, I've been thinking of something a good bit lately."

"Jest thirty-five years, Tony, come next Thanksgiving," replied the old man, promptly, in a thin asthmatic falsetto. "I recollect your mother used to say it dated from the time your Aunt Hannah was here with the girls."

"Yes, father, I think it may be a matter of thirty-five years; though it don't seem so long, does it? But I've been thinking harder for the last week or two, and I'm going to speak out."

Unbounded amazement looked out at the old man's eyes; his tongue, utterly unprepared for the unexpected contingency, refused its office; a corncob imperfectly denuded dropped from his nerveless hand, and was critically examined, in turn, by the gossamer dogs, hoping against hope. A smoking brand in the fireplace fell suddenly upon a bed of hot coals, where, lacking the fortitude of Guatimozin, it emitted a sputtering protest, followed by a thin flame like a visible agony. In the resulting light Tony's haggard face shone competitively with a ruddy blush, which spread over his entire scalp, to the imminent danger of firing his flaxen hair.

"Yes, father," he answered, making a desperate clutch at calmness, but losing his grip, "I'm going to make a clean breast of it this time, for sure! Then you can do what you like about it."

The paternal organ of speech found sufficient strength to grind out an intimation that the paternal ear was open for business.

"I've studied it all over, father; I've looked at it from every side; I've been through it with a lantern! And I've come to the conclusion that, seeing as I'm the oldest, it's about time I was beginning to think of getting married!"

NO CHARGE FOR ATTENDANCE

Near the road leading from Deutscherkirche to Lagerhaus may be seen the ruins of a little cottage. It never was a very pretentious pile, but it has a history. About the middle of the last century it was occupied by one Heinrich Schneider, who was a small farmer—so small a farmer his clothes wouldn't fit him without a good deal of taking-in. But Heinrich Schneider was young. He had a wife, however—most small farmers have when young. They were rather poor: the farm was just large enough to keep them comfortably hungry.

Schneider was not literary in his taste; his sole reading was an old dog's-eared copy of the "Arabian Nights" done into German, and in that he read nothing but the story of "Aladdin and his Wonderful Lamp." Upon his five hundredth perusal of that he conceived a valuable idea: he would rub *his* lamp and *corral* a Genie! So he put a thick leather glove on his right hand, and went to the cupboard to get out the lamp. He had no lamp. But this disappointment, which would have been instantly fatal to a more despondent man, was only an agreeable stimulus to him. He took out an old iron candle-snuffer, and went to work upon that.

Now, iron is very hard; it requires more rubbing than any other metal. I once chafed a Genie out of an anvil, but I was quite weary before I got him all out; the slightest irritation of a leaden water-pipe would have fetched the same Genie out of it like a rat from his hole. But having planted all his poultry, sown his potatoes, and set out his wheat, Heinrich had the whole summer before him, and he was patient; he devoted all his time to compelling the attendance of the Supernatural.

When the autumn came, the good wife reaped the chickens, dug out the apples, plucked the pigs and other cereals; and a wonderfully abundant harvest it was. Schneider's crops had flourished amazingly. That was because he did not worry them all summer with agricultural implements. One evening when the produce had been stored, Heinrich sat at his fireside operating upon his candle-snuffer with the same simple faith as in the early spring. Suddenly there was a knock at the door, and the expected Genie put in an appearance. His advent begot no little surprise in the good couple.

He was a very substantial incarnation, indeed, of the Supernatural. About eight feet in length, extremely fat, thick-limbed, ill-favoured, heavy of movement, and generally unpretty, he did not at first sight impress his new master any too favourably.

However, he was given a stool at the fireside, and Heinrich plied him with a multitude of questions: Where did he come from? whom had he last served? how did he like Aladdin? and did he think *they* should get on well? To all these queries the Genie returned evasive answers; he was Delphic to the verge of unintelligibility. He would only nod mysteriously, muttering beneath his breath in some unknown tongue, probably Arabic —in which, however, his master thought he could distinguish the words "roast" and "boiled" with significant frequency. This Genie must have served last in the capacity of cook.

This was a gratifying discovery: for the next four months or so there would be nothing to do about the farm; the Slave could prepare the family meals during the winter, and in the spring go regularly to work. Schneider was too shrewd to risk everything by extravagant demands all at once. He remembered the roc's egg of the legend, and thought he would proceed with caution. So the good couple brought out their cooking utensils, and by pantomime inducted the Slave into the mystery of their use. They showed him the larder, the cellars, the granary, the chicken-coops, and everything. He appeared interested and intelligent, apprehended the salient points of the situation with marvellous ease, and nodded like he would drop his big head off—did everything but talk.

After this the *frau* prepared the evening meal, the Genie assisting very satisfactorily, except that his notions of quantity were rather too liberal; perhaps this was natural in one accustomed to palaces and courts. When all was on the table, by way of testing his Slave's obedience Heinrich sat down at the board and carelessly rubbed the candle-snuffer. The Genie was there in a second! Not only so, but he fell upon the viands with an ardour and sincerity that were alarming. In two minutes he had got away with everything on the table. The rapidity with which that spirit crowded all manner of edibles into his neck was simply shocking!

Having finished his repast he stretched himself before the fire and went to sleep. Heinrich and Barbara were depressed in spirit; they sat up until nearly morning in silence, waiting for the Genie to vanish for the night; but he did not perceptibly vanish any. Moreover, he had not vanished next morning; he had risen with the lark, and was preparing breakfast, having made his estimates upon a basis of most immoderate consumption. To this he soon sat down with the same catholicity of appetite that had distinguished him the previous evening. Having bolted this preposterous breakfast he arrayed his fat face in a sable scowl, beat his master with a stewpan, stretched himself before the fire, and again addressed himself to sleep. Over a furtive and clandestine meal in the larder, Heinrich and Barbara confessed themselves thoroughly heart-sick of the Supernatural.

"I told you so," said he; "depend upon it, patient industry is a thousand per cent. better than this invisible agency. I will now take the fatal candle-snuffer a mile from here, rub it real hard, fling it aside, and run away."

But he didn't. During the night ten feet of snow had fallen. It lay all winter too.

Early the next spring there emerged from that cottage by the wayside the unstable framework of a man dragging through seas of melting snow a tottering female of dejected aspect. Forlorn, crippled, famishing, and discouraged, these melancholy relics held on their way until they came to a cross-roads (all leading to Lagerhaus), where they saw clinging to an upright post the tatter of an old placard. It read as follows:

> LOST, strayed, or stolen, from Herr Schaackhofer's Grand Museum, the celebrated Patagonian Giant, Ugolulah. Height 8 ft. 2 in., elegant figure, handsome, intelligent features, sprightly and vivacious in conversation, of engaging address, temperate in diet, harmless and tractable in disposition. Answers to the nickname of Fritz Sneddeker. Any one returning him to Herr Schaackhofer will receive Seven Thalers Reward, and no questions asked.

It was a tempting offer, but they did not go back for the giant. But he was afterwards discovered sleeping sweetly upon the hearthstone, after a hearty meal of empty barrels and boxes. Being secured he was found to be too fat for egress by the door. So the house was pulled down to let him out; and that is how it happens to be in ruins now.

Ambrose Bierce

PERNICKETTY'S FRIGHT

"Ssssst!"

Dan Golby held up his hand to enjoin silence; in a breath we were as quiet as mice. Then it came again, borne upon the night wind from away somewhere in the darkness toward the mountains, across miles of treeless plain—a low, dismal, sobbing sound, like the wail of a strangling child! It was nothing but the howl of a wolf, and a wolf is about the last thing a man who knows the cowardly beast would be afraid of; but there was something so weird and unearthly in this "cry between the silences"—something so banshee-like in its suggestion of the grave—that, old mountaineers that we were, and long familiar with it, we felt an instinctive dread—a dread which was not fear, but only a sense of utter solitude and desolation. There is no sound known to mortal ear that has in it so strange a power upon the imagination as the night-howl of this wretched beast, heard across the dreary wastes of the desert he disgraces.

Involuntarily we drew nearer together, and some one of the party stirred the fire till it sent up a tall flame, widening the black circle shutting us in on all sides. Again rose the faint far cry, and was answered by one fainter and more far in the opposite quarter. Then another, and yet another, struck in—a dozen, a hundred all at once; and in three minutes the whole invisible outer world seemed to consist mainly of wolves, jangled out of tune by some convulsion of nature.

About this time it was a pleasing study to watch the countenance of Old Nick. This party had joined us at Fort Benton, whither he had come on a steamboat, up the Missouri. This was his maiden venture upon the plains, and his habit of querulous faultfinding had, on the first day out, secured him the *sobriquet* of Old Pernicketty, which the attrition of time had worn down to Old Nick. He knew no more of wolves and other animals than a naturalist, and he was now a trifle frightened. He was crouching beside his saddle and kit, listening with all his soul, his hands suspended before him with divergent fingers, his face ashy pale, and his jaw hanging unconsidered below.

Suddenly Dan Golby, who had been watching him with an amused smile, assumed a grave aspect, listened a moment very intently, and remarked:

"Boys, if I didn't *know* those were wolves, I should say we'd better get out of this."

"Eh?" exclaimed Nick, eagerly; "if you did not know they were *wolves*? Why, what else, and what worse, could they be?"

"Well, there's an innocent!" replied Dan, winking slyly at the rest of us. "Why, they *might* be Injuns, of course. Don't you know, you old bummer, that that's the way the red devils run a surprise party? Don't you know that when you hear a parcel of wolves letting on like that, at night, it's a hundred to one they carry bows and arrows?"

Here one or two old hunters on the opposite side of the fire, who had not caught Dan's precautionary wink, laughed good-humouredly, and made derisive comments. At this Dan seemed much vexed, and getting up, he strode over to them to argue it out. It was surprising how easily they were brought round to his way of thinking!

By this time Old Nick was thoroughly perturbed. He fidgeted about, examining his rifle and pistols, tightened his belt, and looked in the direction of his horse. His anxiety became so painful that he did not attempt to conceal it. Upon our part, we affected to partially share it. One of us finally asked Dan if he was quite *sure* they were wolves. Then Dan listened a long time with his ear to the ground, after which he said, hesitatingly:

"Well, no; there's no such thing as *absolute* certainty, I suppose; but I *think* they're wolves. Still, there's no harm in being ready for anything—always well to be ready, I suppose."

Nick needed nothing more; he pounced upon his saddle and bridle, slung them upon his mustang, and had everything snug in less time than it takes to tell it. The rest of the party were far too comfortable to co-operate with Dan to any considerable extent; we contented ourselves with making a show of examining our weapons. All this time the wolves, as is their way when attracted by firelight, were closing in, clamouring like a legion of fiends. If Nick had known that a single pistol-shot would have sent them scampering away for dear life, I presume he would have fired one; as it was, he had Indian on the brain, and just stood by his horse, quaking till his teeth rattled like dice in a box.

"No," pursued the implacable Dan, "these *can't* be Injuns; for if they were, we should, perhaps, hear an owl or two among them. The chiefs sometimes hoot, owl-fashion, just to let the rabble know they're standing up to the work like men, and to show where they are."

"Too-hoo-hoo-hoo-hooaw!"

It took us all by surprise. Nick made one spring and came down astride his sleepy mustang, with force enough to have crushed a smaller beast. We all rose to our feet, except Jerry Hunker, who was lying flat on his stomach, with his head buried in his arms, and whom we had thought sound asleep. One look at *him* reassured us as to the "owl" business, and we settled back, each man pretending to his neighbour that he had got up merely for effect upon Nick.

That man was now a sight to see. He sat in his saddle gesticulating wildly, and imploring us to get ready. He trembled like a jelly-fish. He took out his pistols, cocked them, and thrust them so back into the holsters, without knowing what he was about. He cocked his rifle, holding it with the muzzle directed anywhere, but principally our way; grasped his bowie-knife between his teeth, and cut his tongue trying to talk; spurred his nag into the fire, and backed him out across our blankets; and finally sat still, utterly unnerved, while we roared with the laughter we could no longer suppress.

Hwissss! pft! swt! cheew! Bones of Caesar! The arrows flitted and clipt amongst us like a flight of bats! Dan Golby threw a double-summersault, alighting on his head. Dory Durkee went smashing into the fire. Jerry Hunker was pinned to the sod where he lay fast asleep. Such dodging and ducking, and clawing about for weapons I never saw. And such genuine Indian yelling—it chills my marrow to write of it!

Old Nick vanished like a dream; and long before we could find our tools and get to work we heard the desultory reports of his pistols exploding in his holsters, as his pony measured off the darkness between us and safety.

For some fifteen minutes we had tolerable warm work of it, individually, collectively, and miscellaneously; single-handed, and one against a dozen; struggling with painted savages in the firelight, and with one another in the dark; shooting the living, and stabbing the dead; stampeding our horses, and fighting *them*; battling with anything that would battle, and smashing our gunstocks on whatever would not!

When all was done—when we had renovated our fire, collected our horses, and got our dead into position—we sat down to talk it over. As we sat there, cutting up our clothing for bandages, digging the poisoned arrow-heads out of our limbs, readjusting our scalps, or swapping them for such vagrant ones as there was nobody to identify, we could not help smiling to think how we had frightened Old Nick. Dan Golby, who was sinking rapidly, whispered that "it was the one sweet memory he had to sustain and cheer him in crossing the dark river into everlasting f—." It is uncertain how Dan would have finished that last word; he may have meant "felicity"—he may have meant "fire." It is nobody's business.

JUNIPER

He was a dwarf, was Juniper. About the time of his birth Nature was executing a large order for prime giants, and had need of all her materials. Juniper infested the wooded interior of Norway, and dwelt in a cave—a miserable hole in which a blind bat in a condition of sempiternal torpor would have declined to hibernate, rent-free. Juniper was such a feeble little wretch, so inoffensive in his way of life, so modest in his demeanour, that every one was disposed to love him like a cousin; there was not enough of him to love like a brother. He, too, was inclined to return the affection; he was too weak to love very hard, but he made the best stagger at it he could. But a singular fatality prevented a perfect communion of soul between him and his neighbours. A strange destiny had thrown its shadow upon him, which made it cool for him in summer. There was a divinity that shaped his ends extremely rough, no matter how he hewed them.

Somewhere in that vicinity lived a monstrous bear—a great hulking obnoxious beast who had no more soul than tail. This rascal had somehow conceived a notion that the appointed function of his existence was the extermination of the dwarf. If you met the latter you might rely with cheerful confidence upon seeing the ferocious brute in eager pursuit of him in less than a minute. No sooner would Juniper fairly accost you, looking timidly over his shoulder the while, than the raging savage would leap out of some contiguous jungle and make after him like a locomotive engine too late for the train. Then poor Juniper would streak it for the nearest crowd of people,

Ambrose Bierce

diving and dodging amongst their shins with nimble skill, shrieking all the time like a panther. He was as earnest about it as if he had made a bet upon the result of the race. Of course everybody was too busy to stop, but in his blind terror the dwarf would single out some luckless wight—commonly some well-dressed person; Juniper instinctively sought the protection of the aristocracy—getting behind him, ducking between his legs, surrounding him, dancing through him—doing anything to save the paltry flitch of his own bacon. Presently the bear would lose all patience and nip the other fellow. Then, ashamed of losing his temper, he would sneak sullenly away, taking along the body. When he had gone, poor Juniper would fall upon his knees, tearing his beard, pounding his breast, and crying *Mea culpa* in deep remorse. Afterwards he would pay a visit of condolence to the bereaved relations and offer to pay the funeral expenses; but of course there never were any funeral expenses. Everybody, as before stated, liked the unhappy dwarf, but nobody liked the company he kept, and people were not at home to him as a rule. Whenever he came into a village traffic was temporarily suspended, and he was made the centre of as broad a solitude as could be hastily improvised.

Many were the attempts to capture the terrible beast; hundreds of the country people would assemble to hunt him with guns and dogs. But even the dogs seemed to have an instinctive sense of some occult connection between him and the dwarf, and could never be made to understand that it was the former that was wanted. Directly they were laid on the scent they would forsake it to invest the dwarf's abode; and it was with much difficulty the pitying huntsmen could induce them to raise the siege. Things went on in this unsatisfactory fashion for years; the population annually decreasing, and Juniper making the most miraculous escapes.

Now there resided in a small village near by, a brace of twins; little orphan girls, named Jalap and Ginseng. Their considerate neighbours had told them such pleasing tales about the bear that they decided to leave the country. So they got their valuables together in a box and set out. They met Juniper! He approached to inform them it was a fine morning, when the great beast of a bear "rose like the steam of rich distilled perfume" from the earth in front of them, and made a mouth at him. Juniper did not run, as might have been expected; he stood for a moment peering into the brute's cavernous jaws, and then flew! He absented himself with such extraordinary nimbleness that after he was a mile distant his image appeared to be standing there yet; and looking back he saw it himself. Baffled of his dwarf, the bear thought he would make a shift to get on, for the present, with an orphan. So he picked up Jalap by her middle, and thoughtfully withdrew.

The thankful but disgusted Ginseng continued her emigration, but soon missed the jewel-box, which in their alarm had been dropped and burst asunder. She did not much care for the jewels, but it contained some valuable papers, among them the "Examiner" (a print which once had the misfortune to condemn a book written by the author of this tale) and this she doted on. Returning for her property, she peered cautiously around the angle of a rock, and saw a spectacle that begot in her mind a languid interest. The bear had returned upon a similar mission; he was calmly distending his cheeks with the contents of the broken box. And perched on a rock near at hand sat Juniper waiting for him!

It was natural that a suspicion of collusion between the two should dawn upon that infant's mind. It did dawn; it brightend and broadened into the perfect day of conviction. It was a revelation to the child. "At that moment," said she afterwards, "I felt that I could lay my finger on the best-trained bear in Christendom." But with praiseworthy moderation she controlled herself and didn't do it; she just stood still and allowed the beast to proceed. Having stored all the jewels in his capacious mouth, he began taking in the valuable papers. First some title-deeds disappeared; then some railway bonds; presently a roll of rent-receipts. All these seemed to be as honey to his tongue; he smiled a smile of tranquil happiness. Finally the newspaper vanished into his face like a wisp of straw drawn into a threshing machine.

Then the brute expanded his mouth with a ludicrous gape, spilling out the jewels, a glittering shower. Then he snapped his jaws like a steel trap afflicted with *tetanus*, and stood on his head awhile. Next he made a feeble endeavour to complicate the relations between his parts—to tie himself into a love-knot. Failing in this he lay flat upon his side, wept, retched, and finally, fashioning his visage into the semblance of sickly grin, gave up the ghost. I don't know what he died of; I suppose it was hereditary in his family.

The guilty come always to grief. Juniper was arrested, charged with conspiracy to kill, tried, convicted, sentenced to be hanged, and before the sun went down was pardoned. In searching his cavern the police discovered countless human bones, much torn clothing, and a mighty multitude of empty purses. But nothing of any value—not an article of any value. It was a mystery what Juniper had done with his ill-gotten valuables. The police confessed it was a mystery!

FOLLOWING THE SEA

At the time of "the great earthquake of '68," I was at Arica, Peru. I have not a map by me, and am not certain that Arica is not in Chili, but it can't make much difference; there was earthquake all along there. As nearly as I can remember it occured in August—about the middle of August, 1869 or '70.

Sam Baxter was with me; I think we had gone from San Francisco to make a railway, or something. On the morning of the 'quake, Sam and I had gone down to the beach to bathe. We had shed our boots and begun to moult, when there was a slight tremor of the earth, as if the elephant who supports it were pushing upwards, or lying down and getting up again. Next, the surges, which were flattening themselves upon the sand and dragging away such small trifles as they could lay hold of, began racing out seaward, as if they had received a telegraphic dispatch that somebody was not expected to live. This was needless, for *we* did not expect to live.

When the sea had receded entirely out of sight, we started after it; for it will be remembered we had come to bathe; and bathing without some kind of water is not refreshing in a hot climate. I have heard that bathing in asses' milk is invigorating, but at that time I had no dealings with other authors. I have had no dealings with them since.

For the first four or five miles the walking was very difficult, although the grade was tolerably steep. The ground was soft, there were tangled forests of sea-weed, old rotting ships, rusty

Ambrose Bierce

anchors, human skeletons, and a multitude of things to impede the pedestrian. The floundering sharks bit our legs as we toiled past them, and we were constantly slipping down upon the flat fish strewn about like orange-peel on a sidewalk. Sam, too, had stuffed his shirt-front with such a weight of Spanish doubloons from the wreck of an old galleon, that I had to help him across all the worst places. It was very dispiriting.

Presently, away on the western horizon, I saw the sea coming back. It occurred to me then that I did not wish it to come back. A tidal wave is nearly always wet, and I was now a good way from home, with no means of making a fire.

The same was true of Sam, but he did not appear to think of it in that way. He stood quite still a moment with his eyes fixed on the advancing line of water; then turned to me, saying, very earnestly:

"Tell you what, William; I never wanted a ship so bad from the cradle to the grave! I would give m-o-r-e for a ship!—more than for all the railways and turnpikes you could scare up! I'd give more than a hundred, thousand, million dollars! I would —I'd give all I'm worth, and all my Erie shares, for—just— one—little—ship!"

To show how lightly he could part with his wealth, he lifted his shirt out of his trousers, unbosoming himself of his doubloons, which tumbled about his feet, a golden storm.

By this time the tidal wave was close upon us. Call *that* a wave! It was one solid green wall of water, higher than Niagara Falls, stretching as far as we could see to right and left, without a break in its towering front! It was by no means clear what we ought to do. The moving wall showed no projections by means of which the most daring climber could hope to reach the top. There was no ivy; there were no window-ledges. Stay!—there was the lightning-conductor! No, there wasn't any lightning-conductor. Of course, not!

Looking despairingly upward, I made a tolerably good beginning at thinking of all the mean actions I had wrought in the
flesh, when I saw projecting beyond the crest of the wave a
ship's bowsprit, with a man sitting on it, reading a newspaper!
Thank fortune, we were saved!

Falling upon our knees with tearful gratitude, we got up again
and ran—ran as fast as we could, I suspect; for now the whole
fore-part of the ship bulged through the water directly above
our heads, and might lose its balance any moment. If we had
only brought along our umbrellas!

I shouted to the man on the bowsprit to drop us a line. He
merely replied that his correspondence was already very
onerous, and he hadn't any pen and ink.

Then I told him I wanted to get aboard. He said I would find
one on the beach, about three leagues to the south'ard, where
the "Nancy Tucker" went ashore.

At these replies I was disheartened. It was not so much that the
man withheld assistance, as that he made puns. Presently,
however, he folded his newspaper, put it carefully away in his
pocket, went and got a line, and let it down to us just as we
were about to give up the race. Sam made a lunge at it, and got
it—right into his side! For the fiend above had appended a
shark-hook to the end of the line—which was *his* notion of
humour. But this was no time for crimination and
recrimination. I laid hold of Sam's legs, the end of the rope
was passed about the capstan, and as soon as the men on board
had had a little grog, we were hauled up. I can assure you that
it was no fine experience to go up in that way, close to the
smooth vertical front of water, with the whales tumbling out
all round and above us, and the sword-fishes nosing us
pointedly with vulgar curiosity.

We had no sooner set foot on deck, and got Sam disengaged
from the hook, than the purser stepped up with book and
pencil.

Ambrose Bierce

"Tickets, gentlemen."

We told him we hadn't any tickets, and he ordered us to be set ashore in a boat. It was represented to him that this was quite impossible under the circumstances; but he replied that he had nothing to do with circumstances—did not know anything about circumstances. Nothing would move him till the captain, who was a really kind-hearted man, came on deck and knocked him overboard with a spare topmast. We were now stripped of our clothing, chafed all over with stiff brushes, rolled on our stomachs, wrapped in flannels, laid before a hot stove in the saloon, and strangled with scalding brandy. We had not been wet, nor had we swallowed any sea-water, but the surgeon said this was the proper treatment. I suspect, poor man, he did not often get the opportunity to resuscitate anybody; in fact, he admitted he had not had any such case as ours for years. It is uncertain what he might have done to us if the tender-hearted captain had not thrashed him into his cabin with a knotted hawser, and told us to go on deck.

By this time the ship was passing above the town of Arica, and the sailors were all for'd, sitting on the bulwarks, snapping peas and small shot at the terrified inhabitants flitting through the streets a hundred feet below. These harmless projectiles rattled very merrily upon the upturned boot-soles of the fleeting multitude; but not seeing any fun in this, we were about to go astern and fish a little, when the ship grounded on a hill-top. The captain hove out all the anchors he had about him; and when the water went swirling back to its legal level, taking the town along for company, there we were, in the midst of a charming agricultural country, but at some distance from any sea-port.

At sunrise next morning we were all on deck. Sam sauntered aft to the binnacle, cast his eye carelessly upon the compass, and uttered an ejaculation of astonishment.

"Tell *you*, captain," he called out, "this has been a direr convulsion of nature than you have any idea. Everything's been screwed right round. Needle points due south!"

"Why, you cussed lubber!" growled the skipper, moving up and taking a look, "it p'ints d'rectly to labbard, an' there's the sun, dead ahead!"

Sam turned and confronted him, with a steady gaze of ineffable contempt.

"Now, who said it wasn't dead ahead?—tell me *that*. Shows how much *you* know about earthquakes. 'Course, I didn't mean just this continent, nor just this earth: I tell you, the *whole thing's* turned!"

A TALE OF SPANISH VENGEANCE

Don Hemstitch Blodoza was an hidalgo—one of the highest dalgos of old Spain. He had a comfortably picturesque castle on the Guadalquiver, with towers, battlements, and mortages on it; but as it belonged, not to his own creditors, but to those of his bitterest enemy, who inhabited it, Don Hemstitch preferred the forest as a steady residence. He had that curse of Spanish pride which will not permit one to be a burden upon the man who may happen to have massacred all one's relations, and set a price upon the heads of one's family generally. He had made a vow never to accept the hospitality of Don Symposio—not if he died for it. So he pervaded the romantic dells, and the sunless jungle was infected with the sound of his guitar. He rose in the morning and laved him in the limpid brooklet; and the beams of the noonday sun fell upon him in the pursuit of diet—

"The thistle's downy seed his fare,
His drink the morning dew."

He throve but indifferently upon this meagre regimen, but beyond all other evils a true Spaniard of the poorer sort dreads obesity. During the darkest night of the season he will get up at an absurd hour and stab his best friend in the back rather than grow fat.

It will of course be suspected by the experienced reader that Don Hemstitch did not have any bed. Like the Horatian lines above quoted—

"He perched at will on every spray."

In translating this tale into the French, M. Victor Hugo will please twig the proper meaning of the word "spray"; I shall be very angry if he make it appear that my hero is a gull.

One morning while Don Hemstitch was dozing upon his leafy couch—not his main couch, but a branch—he was roused from his tranquil nap by the grunting of swine; or, if you like subtle distinctions, by the sound of human voices. Peering cautiously through his bed-hangings, he saw below him at a little distance two of his countrymen in conversation. The fine practised phrenzy of their looks, their excellently rehearsed air of apprehensive secrecy, showed him they were merely conspiring against somebody's life; and he dismissed the matter from his mind until the mention of his own name recalled his attention. One of the conspirators was urging the other to make one of a joint-stock company for the Don's assassination; but the more conscientious plotter would not consent.

"The laws of Spain," said the latter, "with which we have an acquaintance meanly withheld from the attorneys, enjoin that when one man murders another, except for debt, he must make provision for the widow and orphans. I leave it to you if, after the summer's unprofitable business, we are in a position to assume the care and education of a large family. We have not a single asset, and our liabilities amount to fourteen widows, and more than thirty children of strong and increasing appetite.

"*Car-r-rajo!*" hissed the other through his beard; "we will slaughter the lot of them!"

At this cold-blooded proposition his merciful companion recoiled aghast.

"*Diablo!*" he shrieked. "Tempt me no farther. What! immolate a whole hecatomb of guiltless women and children? Consider the funeral expense!"

There is really no moving the law-abiding soul to crime of doubtful profit. But Don Hemstitch was not at ease; he could not say how soon it might transpire that he had nor chick nor child. Should Don Symposio pass that way and communicate this information—and he was in a position to know—the moral scruples of the conscientious plotter would vanish like the baseless fabric of a beaten cur. Moreover, it is always unpleasant to be included in a conspiracy in which one is not a conspirator. Don Hemstitch resolved to sell his life at the highest market price.

Hastily descending his tree, he wrapped his cloak about him and stood for some time, wishing he had a poniard. Trying the temper of this upon his thumbnail, he found it much more amiable than his own. It was a keen Toledo blade—keen enough to sever a hare. To nerve himself for the deadly work before him, he began thinking of a lady whom he had once met—the lovely Donna Lavaca, beloved of El Toro-blanco. Having thus wrought up his Castilian soul to a high pitch of jealously, he felt quite irresistible, and advanced towards the two ruffians with his poniard deftly latent in his flowing sleeve. His mien was hostile, his stride puissant, his nose tip-tilted— not to put too fine a point upon it, petallic. Don Hemstitch was upon the war-path with all his might. The forest trembled as he trode, the earth bent like thin ice beneath his heel. Birds, beasts, serpents, and poachers fled affrighted to the right and left of his course. He came down upon the unsuspecting assassins like a mild Spanish avalanche.

"*Senores!*" he thundered, with a frightful scowl and a faint aroma of garlic, "patter your *pater-nosters* as fast as you conveniently may. You have but ten minutes to exist. Has either of you a watch?"

Then might you have seen a guilty dismay over-spreading the faces of two sinners, like a sudden snow paling twin mountain peaks. In the presence of Death, Crime shuddered and sank into his boots. Conscience stood appalled in the sight of Retribution. In vain the villains essayed speech; each palsied tongue beat out upon the yielding air some weak words of supplication, then clave to its proper concave. Two pairs of brawny knees unsettled their knitted braces, and bent limply beneath their loads of incarnate wickedness swaying unsteadily above. With clenched hands and streaming eyes these wretched men prayed silently. At this supreme moment an American gentleman sitting by, with his heels upon a rotted oaken stump, tilted back his chair, laid down his newspaper, and began operating upon a half-eaten apple-pie. One glance at the title of that print—one look at that calm angular face clasped in its crescent of crisp crust—and Don Hemstitch Blodoza reeled, staggered like an exhausted spinning-top. He spread his baffled hand upon his eyes, and sank heavily to earth!

"Saved! saved!" shrieked the penitent conspirators, springing to their feet. The far deeps of the forest whispered in consultation, and a distant hillside echoed back the words. "Saved!" sang the rocks—"Saved!" the glad birds twittered from the leaves above. The hare that Don Hemstitch Blodoza's poniard would have severed limped awkwardly but confidently about, saying, "Saved!" as well as he knew how.

Explanation is needless. The American gentleman was the Special Correspondent of the "New York Herald." It is tolerably well known that except beneath his searching eye no considerable event can occur—and his whole attention was focused upon that apple-pie!

That is how Spanish vengeance was balked of its issue.

MRS. DENNISON'S HEAD

While I was employed in the Bank of Loan and Discount (said Mr. Applegarth, smiling the smile with which he always prefaced a nice old story), there was another clerk there, named Dennison—a quiet, reticent fellow, the very soul of truth, and a great favourite with us all. He always wore crape on his hat, and once when asked for whom he was in mourning he replied his wife, and seemed much affected. We all expressed our sympathy as delicately as possible, and no more was said upon the subject. Some weeks after this he seemed to have arrived at that stage of tempered grief at which it becomes a relief to give sorrow words—to speak of the departed one to sympathizing friends; for one day he voluntarily began talking of his bereavement, and of the terrible calamity by which his wife had been deprived of her head!

This sharpened our curiosity to the keenest edge; but of course we controlled it, hoping he would volunteer some further information with regard to so singular a misfortune; but when day after day went by and he did not allude to the matter, we got worked up into a fever of excitement about it. One evening after Dennison had gone, we held a kind of political meeting about it, at which all possible and impossible methods of decapitation were suggested as the ones to which Mrs. D. probably owed her extraordinary demise. I am sorry to add that we so far forgot the grave character of the event as to lay small wagers that it was done this way or that way; that it was accidental or premeditated; that she had had a hand in it herself or that it was wrought by circumstances beyond her control. All was mere conjecture, however; but from that time Dennison, as the custodian of a secret upon which we had staked our cash, was an object of more than usual interest. It wasn't entirely that, either; aside from our paltry wagers, we felt a consuming curiosity to know the truth for its own sake. Each set himself to work to elicit the dread secret in some way; and the misdirected ingenuity we developed was wonderful. All sorts of pious devices were resorted to to entice poor Dennison into clearing up the mystery. By a thousand indirect methods we sought to entrap him into divulging all. History, fiction, poesy—all were laid under contribution, and from Goliah down, through Charles I., to Sam Spigger, a local celebrity who got his head entangled in mill machinery, every one who had ever mourned the loss of a head received his due share of attention during office hours. The regularity with which we introduced, and the pertinacity with which we stuck to, this one topic came near getting us all discharged; for one day the cashier came out of his private office and intimated that if we valued our situations the subject of hanging would afford us the means of retaining them. He added that he always selected his subordinates with an eye to their conversational abilities, but variety of subject was as desirable, at times, as exhaustive treatment.

During all this discussion Dennison, albeit he had evinced from the first a singular interest in the theme, and shirked not his fair share of the conversation, never once seemed to understand that it had any reference to himself. His frank truthful nature was quite unable to detect the personal significance of the subject. It was plain that nothing short of a definite inquiry would elicit the information we were dying to obtain; and at a "caucus," one evening, we drew lots to determine who should openly propound it. The choice fell upon me.

Next morning we were at the bank somewhat earlier than usual, waiting impatiently for Dennison and the time to open the doors: they always arrived together. When Dennison stepped into the room, bowing in his engaging manner to each clerk as he passed to his own desk, I confronted him, shaking him warmly by the hand. At that moment all the others fell to writing and figuring with unusual avidity, as if thinking of anything under the sun except Dennison's wife's head.

"Oh, Dennison," I began, as carelessly as I could manage it; "speaking of decapitation reminds me of something I would like to ask you. I have intended asking it several times, but it has always slipped my memory. Of course you will pardon me if it is not a fair question."

As if by magic, the scratching of pens died away, leaving a dead silence which quite disconcerted me; but I blundered on:

"I heard the other day—that is, you said—or it was in the newspapers—or somewhere—something about your poor wife, you understand—about her losing her head. Would you mind telling me how such a distressing accident—if it was an accident—occurred?"

When I had finished, Dennison walked straight past me as if he didn't see me, went round the counter to his stool, and perched himself gravely on the top of it, facing the other clerks. Then he began speaking, calmly, and without apparent emotion:

"Gentlemen, I have long desired to speak of this thing, but you gave me no encouragement, and I naturally supposed you were indifferent. I now thank you all for the friendly interest you take in my affairs. I will satisfy your curiosity upon this point at once, if you will promise never hereafter to allude to the matter, and to ask not a single question now."

We all promised upon our sacred honour, and collected about him with the utmost eagerness. He bent his head a moment, then raised it, quietly saying:

"My poor wife's head was bitten off!"

"By what?" we all exclaimed eagerly, with suspended breath.

He gave us a look full of reproach, turned to his desk, and went at his work.

We went at ours.

Ambrose Bierce

A FOWL WITCH

Frau Gaubenslosher was strongly suspected of witchcraft. I don't think she was a witch, but would not like to swear she was not, in a court of law, unless a good deal depended upon my testimony, and I had been properly suborned beforehand. A great many persons accused of witchcraft have themselves stoutly disbelieved the charge, until, when subjected to shooting with a silver bullet or boiling in oil, they have found themselves unable to endure the test. And it must be confessed appearances were against the Frau. In the first place, she lived quite alone in a forest, and had no visiting list. This was suspicious. Secondly—and it was thus, mainly, that she had acquired her evil repute—all the barn-yard fowls in the vicinity seemed to bear her the most uncompromising ill-will. Whenever she passed a flock of hens, or ducks, or turkeys, or geese, one of them, with dropped wings, extended neck, and open bill, would start in hot pursuit. Sometimes the whole flock would join in for a few moments with shrill clamour; but there would always be one fleeter and more determined than the rest, and that one would keep up the chase with unflagging zeal clean out of sight.

Upon these occasions the dame's fright was painful to behold. She would not scream—her organs of screech seemed to have lost their power—nor, as a rule, would she curse; she would just address herself to silent prayerful speed, with every symptom of abject terror!

The Frau's explanation of this unnatural persecution was

singularly weak. Upon a certain night long ago, said she, a poor bedraggled and attenuated gander had applied at her door for relief. He stated in piteous accents that he had eaten nothing for months but tin-tacks and an occasional beer-bottle; and he had not roosted under cover for so long a time he did not know what it was like. Would she give him a place on her fender, and fetch out six or eight cold pies to amuse him while she was preparing his supper? To this plea she turned a deaf ear, and he went away. He came again the next night, however, bringing a written certificate from a clergyman that his case was a deserving one. She would not aid him, and he departed. The night after he presented himself again, with a paper signed by the relieving officer of the parish, stating that the necessity for help was most urgent.

By this time the Frau's good-nature was quite exhausted: she slew him, dressed him, put him in a pot, and boiled him. She kept him boiling for three or four days, but she did not eat him because her teeth were just like anybody's teeth—no weaker, perhaps, but certainly no stronger nor sharper. So she fed him to a threshing machine of her acquaintance, which managed to masticate some of the more modern portions, but was hopelessly wrecked upon the neck. From that time the poor beldame had lived under the ban of a great curse. Hens took after her as naturally as after the soaring beetle; geese pursued her as if she were a fleeting tadpole; ducks, turkeys, and guinea fowl camped upon her trail with tireless pertinacity.

Now there was a leaven of improbability in this tale, and it leavened the whole lump. Ganders do not roost; there is not one in a hundred of them that could sit on a fender long enough to say Jack Robinson. So, as the Frau lived a thousand years before the birth of common sense—say about a half century ago—when everything uncommon had a smell of the supernatural, there was nothing for it but to consider her a witch. Had she been very feeble and withered, the people would have burned her, out of hand; but they did not like to proceed to extremes without perfectly legal evidence. They

Ambrose Bierce

were cautious, for they had made several mistakes recently. They had sentenced two or three females to the stake, and upon being stripped the limbs and bodies of these had not redeemed the hideous promise of their shrivelled faces and hands. Justice was ashamed of having toasted comparatively plump and presumably innocent women; and the punishment of this one was wisely postponed until the proof should be all in.

But in the meantime a graceless youth, named Hans Blisselwartle, made the startling discovery that none of the fowls that pursued the Frau ever came back to boast of it. A brief martial career seemed to have weaned them from the arts of peace and the love of their kindred. Full of unutterable suspicion, Hans one day followed in the rear of an exciting race between the timorous dame and an avenging pullet. They were too rapid for him; but bursting suddenly in at the lady's door some fifteen minutes afterward, he found her in the act of placing the plucked and eviscerated Nemesis upon her cooking range. The Frau betrayed considerable confusion; and although the accusing Blisselwartle could not but recognize in her act a certain poetic justice, he could not conceal from himself that there was something grossly selfish and sordid in it. He thought it was a good deal like bottling an annoying ghost and selling him for clarified moonlight; or like haltering a nightmare and putting her to the cart.

When it transpired that the Frau ate her feathered persecutors, the patience of the villagers refused to honour the new demand upon it: she was at once arrested, and charged with prostituting a noble superstition to a base selfish end. We will pass over the trial; suffice it she was convicted. But even then they had not the heart to burn a middle-aged woman, with full rounded outlines, as a witch, so they broke her upon the wheel as a thief.

The reckless antipathy of the domestic fowls to this inoffensive lady remains to be explained. Having rejected her theory, I am bound in honour to set up one of my own. Happily an inventory of her effects, now before me, furnishes a tolerably safe basis. Amongst the articles of personal property I note "One long, thin, silken fishing line, and hook." Now if I were a barn-yard fowl—say a goose—and a lady not a friend of mine were to pass me, munching sweetmeats, and were to drop a nice fat worm, passing on apparently unconscious of her loss, I think I should try to get away with that worm. And if after swallowing it I felt drawn towards that lady by a strong personal attachment, I suppose that I should yield if I could not help it. And then if the lady chose to run and I chose to follow, making a good deal of noise, I suppose it would look as if I were engaged in a very reprehensible pursuit, would it not? With the light I have, that is the way in which the case presents itself to my intelligence; though, of course, I may be wrong.

Ambrose Bierce

THE CIVIL SERVICE IN FLORIDA

Colonel Bulper was of a slumberous turn. Most people are not: they work all day and sleep all night—are always in one or the other condition of unrest, and never slumber. Such persons, the Colonel used to remark, are fit only for sentry duty; they are good to watch our property while we take our rest—and they take the property. But this tale is not of them; it is of Colonel Bulper.

There was a fellow named Halsey, a practical joker, and one of the most disagreeable of his class. He would remain broad awake for a year at a time, for no other purpose than to break other people of their natural rest. And I must admit that from the wreck of his faculties upon the rock of *insomnia* he had somehow rescued a marvellous ingenuity and fertility of expedient. But this tale is not so much of him as of Colonel Bulper.

At the time of which I write, the Colonel was the Collector of Customs at a sea-port town in Florida, United States. The climate there is perpetual summer; it never rains, nor anything; and there was no good reason why the Colonel should not have enjoyed it to the top of his bent, as there was enough for all. In point of fact, the Collectorship had been given him solely that he might repair his wasted vitality by a short season of unbroken repose; for during the Presidential canvass immediately preceding his appointment he had been kept awake a long time by means of strong tea, in order to deliver an able and exhaustive political argument prepared by the candidate, who was ultimately successful in spite of it. Halsey, who had favoured the other aspirant, was a merchant, and had nothing in the world to do but annoy the collector. If the latter could have kept away from him, the dignity of the office might have been preserved, and the object of the incumbent's appointment to it attained; but sneak away whithersoever he might—into the heart of the dismal swamp, or anywhere in the Everglades—some vagrom Indian or casual negro was sure to stumble over him before long, and go and tell Halsey, securing a plug of tobacco for reward. Or if he was not found in this way, some company was tolerably certain, in the course of time, to survey a line of railway athwart his leafy couch, and laying his prostrate trunk aside out of the way, send word to his persecutor; who, as soon as the line was as nearly completed as it ever would be, would come down on horseback with some diabolical device for waking the slumberer. I will confess there is a subtle seeming of unlikelihood about all this; but in the land where Ponce de Leon searched for the Fountain of Youth there is an air of unreality in everything. I can only say I have had the story by me a long time, and it seems to me just as true as it was the day I wrote it.

Sometimes the Colonel would seek out a hillside with a southern exposure; but no sooner would he compose his members for a bit of slumber, than Halsey would set about making inquiries for him, under pretence that a ship was *en route* from Liverpool, and the collector's signature might be required for her anchoring papers. Having traced him—which, owing to the meddlesome treachery of the venal natives, he was always able to do—Halsey would set off to Texas for a seed of the prickly pear, which he would plant exactly beneath the slumberer's body. This he called a triumph of modern engineering! As soon as the young vegetable had pushed its spines above the soil, of course the Colonel would have to get up and seek another spot—and this nearly always waked him.

Upon one occasion the Colonel existed five consecutive days without slumber—travelling all day and sleeping in the weeds at night—to find an almost inaccessible crag, on the summit of

Ambrose Bierce

which he hoped to be undisturbed until the action of the dew should wear away the rock all round his body, when he expected and was willing to roll off and wake. But even there Halsey found him out, and put eagles' eggs in his southern pockets to hatch. When the young birds were well grown, they pecked so sharply at the Colonel's legs that he had to get up and wring their necks. The malevolence of people who scorn slumber seems to be practically unlimited.

At last the Colonel resolved upon revenge, and having dreamed out a feasible plan, proceeded to put it into execution. He had in the warehouse some Government powder, and causing a keg of this to be conveyed into his private office, he knocked out the head. He next penned a note to Halsey, asking him to step down to the office "upon important business;" adding in a postscript, "As I am liable to be called out for a few moments at any time, in case you do not find me in, please sit down and amuse yourself with the newspaper until I return." He knew Halsey was at his counting-house, and would certainly come if only to learn what signification a Government official attached to the word "business." Then the Colonel procured a brief candle and set it into the powder. His plan was to light the candle, dispatch a porter with the message, and bolt for home. Having completed his preparations, he leaned back in his easy chair and smiled. He smiled a long time, and even achieved a chuckle. For the first time in his life, he felt a serene sense of happiness in being particularly wide awake. Then, without moving from his chair, he ignited the taper, and put out his hand toward the bell-cord, to summon the porter. At this stage of his vengeance the Colonel fell into a tranquil and refreshing slumber.

*   *   *   *   *

There is nothing omitted here; that is merely the Colonel's present address.

A TALE OF THE BOSPHORUS

Pollimariar was the daughter of a Mussulman—she was, in fact, a Mussulgirl. She lived at Stamboul, the name of which is an admirable rhyme to what Pollimariar was profanely asserted to be by her two sisters, Djainan and Djulya. These were very much older than Pollimariar, and proportionately wicked. In wickedness they could discount her, giving her the first innings.

The relations between Pollimariar and her sisters were in all respects similar to those that existed between Cinderella and *her* sisters. Indeed, these big girls seldom read anything but the story of Cinderella; and that work, no doubt, had its influence in forming their character. They were always apparelling themselves in gaudy dresses from Paris, and going away to balls, leaving their meritorious little sister weeping at home in their every-day finery. Their father was a commercial traveller, absent with his samples in Damascus most of the time; and the poor girl had no one to protect her from the outrage of exclusion from the parties to which she was not invited. She fretted and chafed very much at first, but after forbearance ceased to be a virtue it came rather natural to her to exercise a patient endurance. But perceiving this was agreeable to her sisters she abandoned it, devising a rare scheme of vengeance. She sent to the "Levant Herald" the following "personal" advertisement:

"G.V.—Regent's Canal 10.30 p.m., Q.K.X. is O.K.! With coals at 48 sh-ll-ngs I cannot endure existence without you!

Ask for G-field St-ch. J.G. + ¶ pro rata. B-tty's N-bob P-ckles. Oz-k-r-t! Meet me at the 'Turban and Scimitar,' Bebeck Road, Thursday morning at three o'clock; blue cotton umbrella, wooden shoes, and Ulster overskirt Polonaise all round the bottom.

One Who Wants to Know Yer."

The latter half of this contained the gist of the whole matter; the other things were put in just to prevent the notice from being conspicuously sensible. Next morning, when the Grand Vizier took up his newspaper, he could not help knowing he was the person addressed; and at the appointed hour he kept the tryst. What passed between them the sequel will disclose, if I can think it out to suit me.

Soon afterwards Djainan and Djulya received cards of invitation to a grand ball at the Sultan's palace, given to celebrate the arrival of a choice lot of Circassian beauties in the market. The first thing the wicked sisters did was to flourish these invitations triumphantly before the eyes of Pollimariar, who declared she did not believe a word of it; indeed, she professed such aggressive incredulity that she had to be severely beaten. But she denied the invitations to the last. She thought it was best to deny them.

The invitations stated that at the proper hour the old original Sultana would call personally, and conduct the young ladies to the palace; and she did so. They thought, at the time, she bore a striking resemblance to a Grand Vizier with his beard shaven off, and this led them into some desultory reflections upon the sin of nepotism and family favour at Court; but, like all moral reflections, these came to nothing. The old original Sultana's attire, also, was, with the exception of a reticule and fan, conspicuously epicene; but, in a country where popular notions of sex are somewhat confused, this excited no surprise.

As the three marched off in stately array, poor little deserted Pollimariar stood cowering at one side, with her fingers spread loosely upon her eyes, weeping like—a crocodile. The Sultana said it was late; they would have to make haste. She had not fetched a cab, however, and a recent inundation of dogs very much impeded their progress. By-and-by the dogs became shallower, but it was near eleven o'clock before they arrived at the Sublime Porte—very old and fruity. A janizary standing here split his visage to grin, but it was surprising how quickly the Sultana had his head off.

Pretty soon afterwards they came to a low door, where the Sultana whistled three times and kicked at the panels. It soon yielded, disclosing two gigantic Nubian eunuchs, black as the ace of clubs, who stared at first, but when shown a very cleverly-executed signet-ring of paste, knocked their heads against the ground with respectful violence. Then one of them consulted a thick book, and took from a secret drawer two metal badges numbered 7,394 and 7,395, which he fastened about the necks of the now frightened girls, who had just observed that the Sultana had vanished. The numbers on the badges showed that this would be a very crowded ball.

The other black now advanced with a measuring tape, and began gravely measuring Djainan from head to heel. She ventured to ask the sable guardian with what article of dress she was to be fitted.

"Bedad, thin, av ye must know," said he, grinning, "it is to be a *sack*."

"What! a *sacque* for a ball?"

"Indade, it's right ye are, mavourneen; it is fer a ball—fer a cannon-ball—as will make yer purty body swim to the bothom nately as ony shtone."

And the eunuch toyed lovingly with his measuring-tape, which the wretched girls now observed was singularly like a bow-string.

"O, sister," shrieked Djainan, "this is—"

"O, sister," shrieked Djulya, "this is—"

"That horrid—"

"That horrid—"

"Harem!"

It was even so. A minute later the betrayed maidens were carried, feet-foremost-and-fainting, through a particularly dirty portal, over which gleamed the infernal legend: "Who enters here leaves soap behind!" I wash my hands of them.

Next morning the following "personal" appeared in the "Levant Herald:"

"P-ll-m-r-r.—All is over. The S-lt-n cleared his shelves of the old stock at midnight. If you purchased the Circ-n B-ties with the money I advanced, be sure you don't keep them too long on hand. Prices are sure to fall when I have done buying for the H-r-m. Meet me at time and place agreed upon, and divide profits. G—d V—r."

JOHN SMITH

AN EDITORIAL ARTICLE FROM A JOURNAL.
OF MAY 3rd, A.D. 3873.

At the quiet little village of Smithcester (the ancient London) will be celebrated to-day the twentieth, centennial anniversary of this remarkable man, the foremost figure of antiquity. The recurrence of what, no longer than six centuries ago, was a popular *fete* day, and which even now is seldom allowed to pass without some recognition by those to whom the word liberty means something more precious than gold, is provocative of peculiar emotion. It matters little whether or no tradition has correctly fixed the date of Smith's birth; that he *was* born— that being born he wrought nobly at the work his hand found to do—that by the mere force of his intellect he established our present perfect form of government, under which civilization has attained its highest and ripest development—these are facts beside which a mere question of chronology sinks into insignificance.

That this extraordinary man originated the Smitharchic system of government is, perhaps, open to honest doubt; very possibly it had a *de facto* existence in various debased and uncertain shapes as early as the sixteenth century. But that he cleared it of its overlying errors and superstitions, gave it a definite form, and shaped it into an intelligible scheme, there is the strongest evidence in the fragments of twentieth-century literature that have descended to us, disfigured though they are with amazingly contradictory statements of his birth, parentage, and

Ambrose Bierce

manner of life before he strode upon the political stage as the liberator of mankind. It is stated that Snakeshear—one of his contemporaries, a poet whose works had in their day some reputation (though it is difficult to say why)—alludes to him as "the noblest Roman of them all;" our ancestors at the time being called Englishmen or Romans, indifferently. In the only fragment of Snakeshear extant, however, we have been unable to find this passage.

Smith's military power is amply attested in an ancient manuscript of undoubted authenticity, which has just been translated from the Japanese. It is an account of the water-battle of Loo, by an eyewitness whose name, unfortunately, has not reached us. In this battle it is stated that Smith overthrew the great Neapolitan general, whom he captured and conveyed in chains to the island of Chickenhurst.

In his Political History of the Twentieth Century, the late Mimble—or, as he would have been called in the time of which he writes, *Mister* Mimble—has this luminous sentence: "With the single exception of Coblentz, there was no European government the Liberator did not upset, and which he did not erect into a pure Smitharchy; and though some of them afterward relapsed temporarily into the crude forms of antiquity, and others fell into fanciful systems begotten of the intellectual activity he had stirred up, yet so firmly did he establish the principle, that in the Thirty-second Century the enlightened world was, what it has since remained, practically Smitharchic."

It may be noted here as a curious coincidence, that the same year which saw the birth of him who established rational government witnessed the death of him who perfected literature. In 1873, Martin Farquhar Tupper—next to Smith the most notable name in history—died of starvation in the streets of London. Like that of Smith, his origin is wrapped in profoundest obscurity. No less than seven British cities claimed the honour of his birth. Meagre indeed is our knowledge of this only bard whose works have descended to us through the changes of twenty centuries entire. All that is positively established is that during his life he was editor of "The Times 'magazine,'" a word of disputed meaning—and, as quaint old Dumbleshaw says, "an accomplished Greek and Latin scholar," whatever "Greek" and "Latin" may have been. Had Smith and Tupper been contemporaries, the iron deeds of the former would doubtless have been immortalized in the golden pages of the latter. Upon such chances does History depend for her materials!

Strangely unimpressible indeed must be the mind which, looking backward through the vista of twenty centuries upon the singular race from whom we are supposed to be descended, can repress a feeling of emotional interest. The names of John Smith and Martin Farquhar Tupper, blazoned upon the page of the dim past, and surrounded by the lesser names of Snakeshear, the first Neapolitan, Oliver Cornwell, Close, "Queen" Elizabeth, or Lambeth, the Dutch Bismarch, Julia Caesar, and a host of contemporary notables are singularly suggestive. They call to mind the odd old custom of covering the body with "clothes;" the curious error of Copernicus and other wide guesses of antique "science;" the lost arts of telegramy, steam locomotion, and printing with movable types; and the exploded theory of gunpowder. They set us thinking upon the zealous idolatry which led men to make pious pilgrimages to the then accessible regions about the North Pole and into the interior of Africa, which at that time was but little better than a wilderness. They conjure up visions of bloodthirsty "Emperors," tyrannical "Kings," vampire "Presidents," and useless "Parliaments"—strangely horrible shapes contrasted with the serene and benevolent aspect of our modern Smithocracy!

Let us to-day rejoice that the old order of things has for ever passed away; let us be thankful that our lot has been cast in more wholesome days than those in which John Smith chalked out the better destinies of a savage race, and Tupper sang divine philosophy to inattentive ears. And yet let us keep green the memory of whatever there was of good—if any—in the

Ambrose Bierce

dark pre-Smithian ages, when men cherished quaint superstitions and rode on the backs of "horses"—when they passed *over* the seas instead of under them—when science had not yet dawned to chase away the shadows of imagination—and when the cabalistic letters A.D., which from habit we still affix to the numerals designating the age of the world, had perhaps a known signification.

SUNDERED HEARTS

Deidrick Schwackenheimer was a lusty young goatherd. He stood six feet two in his *sabots*, and there was not an ounce of superfluous bone or brain in his composition. If he had a fault, it was a tendency to sleep more than was strictly necessary. The nature of his calling fostered this weakness: after being turned into some neighbour's pasture, his animals would not require looking after until the owner of the soil turned them out again. Their guardian naturally devoted the interval to slumber. Nor was there danger of oversleeping: the pitchfork of the irate husbandman always roused him at the proper moment.

At nightfall Deidrick would marshal his flock and drive it homeward to the milking-yard. Here he was met by the fair young Katrina Buttersprecht, the daughter of his employer, who relieved the tense udders of their daily secretion. One evening after the milking, Deidrick, who had for years been nourishing a secret passion for Katrina, was smitten with an idea. Why should she not be his wife? He went and fetched a stool into the yard, led her tenderly to it, seated her, and *asked* her why. The girl thought a moment, and then was at some pains to explain. She was too young. Her old father required all her care. Her little brother would cry. She was engaged to Max Manglewurzzle. She amplified considerably, but these were the essential points of objection. She set them before him *seriatim* with perfect frankness, and without mental reservation. When she had done, her lover, with that instinctive sense of honour characteristic of the true goatherd, made no attempt to alter her decision. Indeed, he had nodded a

Ambrose Bierce

heart-broken assent to each separate proposition, and at the conclusion of the last was fast asleep. The next morning he jocundly drove his goats afield and appeared the same as usual, except that he slept a good deal more, and thought of Katrina a good deal less.

That evening when he returned with his spraddling milch-nannies, he found a second stool placed alongside the first. It was a happy augury; his attentions, then, were not altogether distasteful. He seated himself gravely upon the stool, and when Katrina had done milking, she came and occupied the other. He mechanically renewed his proposal. Then the artless maid proceeded to recapitulate the obstacles to the union. She was too young. Her old father required all her care. Her little brother would cry. She was engaged to Max Manglewurzzle. As each objection was stated and told off on the *frauelein's* fingers, Deidrick nodded a resigned acquiescence, and at the finish was fast asleep. Every evening after that Deidrick proposed in perfect good faith, the girl repeated her objections with equal candour, and they were received with somnolent approval. Love-making is very agreeable, and by the usuage of long years it becomes a confirmed habit. In less than a decade it became impossible for Katrina to enjoy her supper without the regular proposal, and Deidrick could not sleep of a night without the preliminary nap in the goat-yard to taper off his wakefulness. Both would have been wretched had they retired to bed with a shade of misunderstanding between them.

And so the seasons went by. The earth grayed and greened herself anew; the planets sailed their appointed courses; the old goats died, and their virtues were perpetuated in their offspring. Max Manglewurzzle married the miller's daughter; Katrina's little brother, who would have cried at her wedding, did not cry any at his own; the aged Buttersprecht was long gathered to his fathers; and Katrina was herself well stricken in years. And still at fall of night she defined her position to the sleeping lover who had sought her hand—defined it in the self-same terms as upon that eventful eve. The gossiping *frauen* began to whisper it would be a match; but it did not look like it as yet. Slanderous tongues even asserted that it ought to have been a match long ago, but I don't see how it could have been, without the girl's consent. The parish clerk began to hanker after his fee; but, lacking patience, he was unreasonable.

The whole countryside was now taking a deep interest in the affair. The aged did not wish to die without beholding the consummation of the love they had seen bud in their youth; and the young did not wish to die at all. But no one liked to interfere; it was feared that counsel to the woman would be rejected, and a thrashing to the man would be misunderstood. At last the parson took heart of grace to make or mar the match. Like a reckless gambler he staked his fee upon the cast of a die. He went one day and removed the two stools—now worn extremely thin—to another corner of the milking-yard.

That evening, when the distended udders had been duly despoiled, the lovers repaired to their trysting-place. They opened their eyes a bit to find the stools removed. They were tormented with a vague presentiment of evil, and stood for some minutes irresolute; then, assisted to a decision by their weakening knees, they seated themselves flat upon the ground. Deidrick stammered a weak proposal, and Katrina essayed an incoherent objection. But she trembled and became unintelligible; and when he attempted to throw in a few nods of generous approval they came in at the wrong places. With one accord they arose and sought their stools. Katrina tried it again. She succeeded in saying her father was over-young to marry, and Max Manglewurzzle would cry if she took care of him. Deidrick executed a reckless nod that made his neck snap, and was broad awake in a minute. A second time they arose. They conveyed the stools back to their primitive position, and began again. She remarked that her little brother was too old to require all her care, and Max would cry to marry her father. Deidrick addressed himself to sleep, but a horrid nightmare galloped rough-shod into his repose and set him off with a strangled snort. The good understanding between those two hearts was for ever dissipated; neither one knew if the other were afoot or on horseback. Like the sailor's thirtieth stroke with the rope's-end, it was perfectly disgusting! Their meetings after this were so embarrassing that they soon ceased meeting altogether. Katrina died soon after, a miserable broken-spirited maiden of sixty; and Deidrick drags out a wretched existence in a remote town, upon an income of eight *silbergroschen* a week.

Oh, friends and brethren, if you did but know how slight an act may sunder for ever the bonds of love—how easily one may wreck the peace of two faithful hearts—how almost without an effort the waters of affection may be changed to gall and bitterness—I suspect you would make even more more mischief than you do now.

THE EARLY HISTORY OF BATH

Bladud was the eldest son of a British King (whose name I perfectly remember, but do not choose to write) *temp*. Solomon—who does not appear to have known Bladud, however. Bladud was, therefore, Prince of Wales. He was more than that: he was a leper—had it very bad, and the Court physician, Sir William Gull, frequently remarked that the Prince's death was merely a question of time. When a man gets to that stage of leprosy he does not care much for society, particularly if no one will have anything to do with him. So Bladud bade a final adieu to the world, and settled in Liverpool. But not agreeing with the climate, he folded his tent into the shape of an Arab, as Longfellow says, and silently stole away to the southward, bringing up in Gloucestershire.

Here Bladud hired himself out to a farmer named Smith, as a swineherd. But Fate, as he expressed it in the vernacular, was "ferninst him." Leprosy is a contagious disease, within certain degrees of consanguinity, and by riding his pigs afield he communicated it to them; so that in a few weeks, barring the fact that they were hogs, they were no better off than he. Mr. Smith was an irritable old gentleman, so choleric he made his bondsmen tremble—though he was now abroad upon his own recognizances. Dreading his wrath, Bladud quitted his employ, without giving the usual week's notice, but so far conforming to custom in other respects as to take his master's pigs along with him.

We find him next at a place called Swainswick—or

Swineswig—a mile or two to the north-east of Bath, which, as yet, had no existence, its site being occupied by a smooth level reach of white sand, or a stormy pool of black water, travellers of the time disagree which. At Swainswick Bladud found his level; throwing aside all such nonsense as kingly ambition, and the amenities of civilized society—utterly ignoring the deceitful pleasures of common sense—he contented his simple soul with composing *bouts rimes* for Lady Miller, at Batheaston Villa; that one upon a buttered muffin, falsely ascribed by Walpole to the Duchess of Northumberland, was really constructed by Bladud.

A brief glance at the local history of the period cannot but prove instructive. Ralph Allen was then residing at Sham Castle, where Pope accused him of doing good like a thief in the night and blushing to find it unpopular. Fielding was painfully evolving "Tom Jones" from an inner consciousness that might have been improved by soap and any water but that of Bath. Bishop Warburton had just shot the Count Du Barre in a duel with Lord Chesterfield; and Beau Nash was disputing with Dr. Johnson, at the Pelican Inn, Walcot, upon a question of lexicographical etiquette. It is necessary to learn these things in order the better to appreciate the interest of what follows.

During all this time Bladud never permitted his mind to permanently desert his calling; he found family matters a congenial study, and he thought of his swine a good deal, off and on. One day while baiting them amongst the hills, he observed a cloud of steam ascending from the valley below. Having always believed steam a modern invention, this ancient was surprised, and when his measly charge set up a wild squeal, rushing down a steep place into the aspiring vapour, his astonishment ripened into dismay. As soon as he conveniently could Bladud followed, and there he heard the saw—I mean he saw the herd wallowing and floundering multitudinously in a hot spring, and punctuating the silence of nature with grunts of quiet satisfaction, as the leprosy left them and clave to the waters—to which it cleaves yet. It is not probable the pigs went in there for a medicinal purpose; how could they know?

Any butcher will tell you that a pig, after being assassinated, is invariably boiled to loosen the hair. By long usage the custom of getting into hot water has become a habit which the living pig inherits from the dead pork. (See Herbert Spencer on "Heredity.")

Now Bladud (who is said to have studied at Athens, as most Britons of his time did) was a rigid disciple of Bishop Butler; and Butler's line of argument is this: Because a rose-bush blossoms this year, a lamppost will blossom next year. By this ingenious logic he proves the immortality of the human soul, which is good of him; but in so doing he proves, also, the immortality of the souls of snakes, mosquitos, and everything else, which is less commendable. Reasoning by analogy, Bladud was convinced that if these waters would cure a pig, they would cure a prince: and without waiting to see *how* they had cured the bacon, he waded in.

When asked the next day by Sir William Waller if he intended trying the waters again, and if he retained his fondness for that style of bathing, he replied, "Not any, thank you; I am quite cured!" Sir William at once noised abroad the story of the wonderful healing, and when it reached the king's ears, that potentate sent for Bladud to "come home at once and succeed to the throne, just the same as if he had a skin"—which Bladud did. Some time afterwards he thought to outdo Daedalus and Icarus, by flying from the top of St. Paul's Cathedral. He outdid them handsomely; he fell a good deal harder than they did, and broke his precious neck.

Previously to his melancholy end he built the City of Bath, to commemorate his remarkable cure. He endowed the Corporation with ten millions sterling, every penny of the interest of which is annually devoted to the publication of guide-books to Bath, to lure the unwary invalid to his doom. From motives of mercy the Corporation have now set up a contrivance for secretly extracting the mineral properties of the fluid before it is ladled out, but formerly a great number of strangers found a watery grave.

Ambrose Bierce

If King Bladud was generous to Bath, Bath has been grateful in return. One statue of him adorns the principal street, and another graces the swimming pond, both speaking likenesses. The one represents him as he was before he divided his leprosy with the pigs; the other shows him as he appeared after breaking his neck.

Writing in 1631, Dr. Jordan says: "The baths are bear-gardens, where both sexes bathe promiscuously, while the passers-by pelt them with dead dogs, cats, and pigs; and even human creatures are hurled over the rails into the water." It is not so bad as that now, but lodgings are still held at rates which might be advantageously tempered to the shorn.

I append the result of a chemical analysis I caused to be made of these incomparable Waters, that the fame of their virtues may no longer rest upon the inadequate basis of their observed effects.

One hundred parts of the water contain:

Brandate of Sodium	9.50 parts.
Sulphuretted Hydrogen	3.50 "
Citrate of Magnesia	15.00 "
Calves'-foot Jelly	10.00 "
Protocarbonate of Brass	11.00 "
Nitric Acid	7.50 "
Devonshire Cream	6.00 "
Treaclate of Soap	2.00 "
Robur	3.50 "
Superheated Mustard	11.50 "
Frogs	20.45 "
Traces of Guano, Leprosy, Picallilly, and Scotch Whiskey	.05 "

Temperature of the four baths, 117 degrees each—or 468 altogether.

THE FOLLOWING DORG

Dad Petto, as everybody called him, had a dog, upon whom he lavished an amount of affection which, had it been disbursed in a proper quarter, would have been adequate to the sentimental needs of a dozen brace of lovers. The name of this dog was Jerusalem, but it might more properly have been Dan-to-Beersheba. He was not a fascinating dog to look at; you can buy a handsomer dog in any shop than this one. He had neither a graceful exterior nor an engaging address. On the contrary, his exceptional plainness had passed into a local proverb; and such was the inbred coarseness of his demeanour, that in the dark you might have thought him a politician.

If you will take two very bandy-legged curs, cut one off just abaft the shoulders, and the other immediately forward of the haunches, rejecting the fore-part of the first and the rear portion of the second, you will have the raw material for constructing a dog something like Dad Petto's. You have only to effect a junction between the accepted sections, and make the thing eat.

Had he been favoured with as many pairs of legs as a centipede, Jerusalem would not have differed materially from either of his race; but it was odd to see such a wealth of dog wedded to such a poverty of leg. He was so long that the most precocious pupil of the public schools could not have committed him to memory in a week.

It was beautiful to see Jerusalem rounding the angle of a wall, and turning his head about to observe how the remainder of the procession was coming on. He was once circumnavigating a small out-house, when, catching sight of his own hinder-quarters, he flew into a terrible rage. The sight of another dog always had this effect upon Jerusalem, and more especially when, as in this case, he thought he could grasp an unfair advantage. So Jerusalem took after that retreating foe as hard as ever he could hook it. Round and round he flew, but the faster he went, the more his centrifugal force widened his circle, until he presently lost sight of his enemy altogether. Then he slowed down, determined to accomplish his end by strategy. Sneaking closely up to the wall, he moved cautiously forward, and when he had made the full circuit, he came smack up against his own tail. Making a sudden spring, which must have stretched him like a bit of India-rubber, he fastened his teeth into his ham, hanging on like a country visitor. He felt sure he had nailed the other dog, but he was equally confident the other dog had nailed him; so the problem was simplified to a mere question of endurance—and Jerusalem was an animal of pluck. The grim conflict was maintained all one day—maintained with deathless perseverance, until Dad Petto discovered the belligerent and uncoupled him. Then Jerusalem looked up at his master with a shake of the head, as much as to say: "It's a precious opportune arrival for the other pup; but who took *him* off *me*?"

I don't think I can better illustrate the preposterous longitude of this pet, than by relating an incident that fell under my own observation. I was one day walking along the highway with a friend who was a stranger in the neighbourhood, when a rabbit flashed past us, going our way, but evidently upon urgent business. Immediately upon his heels followed the first instal-ment of Dad Petto's mongrel, enveloped in dust, his jaws distended, the lower one shaving the ground to scoop up the rabbit. He was going at a rather lively gait, but was some time in passing. My friend stood a few moments looking on; then rubbed his eyes, looked again, and finally turned to me, just as the brute's tail flitted by, saying, with a broad stare of astonishment:

"Did you ever see a pack of hounds run so perfectly in line? It beats anything! And the speed, too—they seem fairly blended! If a fellow didn't know better, he would swear there was but a single dog!"

I suppose it was this peculiarity of Jerusalem that had won old Petto's regard. He liked as much of anything as he could have for his money; and the expense of this creature, generally speaking, was no greater than that of a brief succinct bull pup. But there were times when he was costly. All dogs are sometimes "off their feed"—will eat nothing for a whole day but a few ox-tails, a pudding or two, and such towelling as they can pick up in the scullery. When Jerusalem got that way, which, to do him justice, was singularly seldom, it made things awkward in the near future. For in a few days after recovering his passion for food, the effect of his former abstemiousness would begin to reach his stomach; but of course all he could *then* devour would work no immediate relief. This he would naturally attribute to the quality of his fare, and would change his diet a dozen times a day, his *menu* in the twelve working hours comprising an astonishing range of articles, from a wood-saw to a kettle of soft soap—edibles as widely dissimilar as the zenith and the nadir, which, also, he would eat. So catholic an appetite was, of course, exceptional: ordinarily Jerusalem was as narrow and illiberal as the best of us. Give him plenty of raw beef, and he would not unsettle his gastric faith by outside speculation or tentative systems.

I could relate things of this dog by the hour. Such, for example, as his clever device for crossing a railway. He never attempted to do this endwise, like other animals, for the obvious reason that, like every one else, he was unable to make any sense of the time-tables; and unless he should by good luck begin the manoeuvre when a train was said to be due, it was likely he would be abbreviated; for of course no one is idiot enough to cross a railway track when the time-table says it is all clear—at least no one as long as Jerusalem. So he would advance his head to the rails, calling in his outlying convolutions, and straightening them alongside the track, parallel with it; and then at a signal previously agreed upon—a short wild bark—this sagacious dog would make the transit unanimously, as it were. By this method he commonly avoided a quarrel with the engine. Altogether he was a very interesting beast, and his master was fond of him no end. And with the exception of compelling Mr. Petto to remove to the centre of the State to avoid double taxation upon him, he was not wholly unprofitable; for he was the best sheep-dog in the country: he always kept the flock well together by the simple device of surrounding them. Having done so, he would lie down, and eat, and eat, and eat, till there wasn't a sheep left, except a few old rancid ones; and even those he would tear into small spring lambs.

Dad Petto never went anywhere without the superior portion of Jerusalem at his side; and he always alluded to him as "the following dorg." But the beast finally became a great nuisance in Illinois. His body obstructed the roads in all directions; and the Representative of that district in the National Congress was instructed by his constituents to bring in a bill taxing dogs by the linear yard, instead of by the head, as the law then stood. Dad Petto proceeded at once to Washington to "lobby" against the measure. He knew the wife of a clerk in the Bureau of Statistics; armed with this influence he felt confident of success. I was myself in Washington, at the time, trying to secure the removal of a postmaster who was personally obnoxious to me, inasmuch as I had been strongly recommended for the position by some leading citizens, who to their high political characters superadded the more substantial merit of being my relations.

Dad and I were standing, one morning, in front of Willard's Hotel, when he stooped over and began patting Jerusalem on the head. All of a sudden the smiling brute sprang open his mouth and bade farewell to a succession of yells which speedily collected ten thousand miserable office-seekers, and an equal quantity of brigadier-generals, who, all in a breath, inquired who had been stabbed, and what was the name of the lady.

Meantime nothing would pacify the pup; he howled most dismally, punctuating his wails with quick sharp shrieks of mortal agony. More than an hour—more than two hours—we strove to discover and allay the canine grievance, but to no purpose.

Presently one of the hotel pages stepped up to Mr. Petto, handing him a telegraphic dispatch just received. It was dated at his home in Cowville, Illinois, and making allowance for the difference in time, something more than two hours previously. It read as follows:

"A pot of boiling glue has just been upset upon Jerusalem's hind-quarters. Shall I try rhubarb, or let it get cold and chisel it off?

"P.S. He did it himself, wagging his tail in the kitchen. Some Democrat has been bribing that dog with cold victuals.— PENELOPE PETTO."

Then we knew what ailed "the following dorg."

I should like to go on giving the reader a short account of this animal's more striking personal peculiarities, but the subject seems to grow under my hand. The longer I write, the longer he becomes, and the more there is to tell; and after all, I shall not get a copper more for pourtraying all this length of dog than I would for depicting an orbicular pig.

SNAKING

Very talkative people always seemed to me to be divided into two classes—those who lie for a purpose and those who lie for the love of lying; and Sam Baxter belonged, with broad impartiality, to both. With him falsehood was not more frequently a means than an end; for he would not only lie without a purpose but at a sacrifice. I heard him once reading a newspaper to a blind aunt, and deliberately falsifying the market reports. The good old lady took it all in with a trustful faith, until he quoted dried apples at fifty cents a yard for unbolted sides; then she arose and disinherited him. Sam seemed to regard the fountain of truth as a stagnant pool, and himself an angel whose business it was to stand by and trouble the waters.

"You know Ben Dean," said Sam to me one day; "I'm down on that fellow, and I'll tell you why. In the winter of '68 he and I were snaking together in the mountains north of the Big Sandy."

"What do you mean by snaking, Sam?"

"Well, *I* like *that*! Why, gathering snakes, to be sure— rattlesnakes for zoological gardens, museums, and side-shows to circuses. This is how it is done: a party of snakers go up to the mountains in the early autumn, with provisions for all winter, and putting up a snakery at some central point, get to work as soon as the torpid season sets in, and before there is much snow. I presume you know that when the nights begin to get cold, the snakes go in under big flat stones, snuggle together, and lie there frozen stiff until the warm days of spring limber them up for business.

"We go about, raise up the rocks, tie the worms into convenient bundles and carry them to the snakery, where, during the snow season, they are assorted, labelled according to quality, and packed away for transportation. Sometimes a single showman will have as many as a dozen snakers in the mountains all winter.

"Ben and I were out, one day, and had gathered a few sheaves of prime ones, when we discovered a broad stone that showed good indications, but we couldn't raise it. The whole upper part of the mountain seemed to be built mostly upon this one stone. There was nothing to be done but mole it—dig under, you know; so taking the spade I soon widened the hole the creatures had got in at, until it would admit my body. Crawling in, I found a kind of cell in the solid rock, stowed nearly full of beautiful serpents, some of them as long as a man. You would have revelled in those worms! They were neatly disposed about the sides of the cave, an even dozen in each berth, and some odd ones swinging from the ceiling in hammocks, like sailors. By the time I had counted them roughly, as they lay, it was dark, and snowing like the mischief. There was no getting back to head-quarters that night, and there was room for but one of us inside."

"Inside what, Sam?"

"See here! have you been listening to what I'm telling you, or not? There is no use telling *you* anything. Perhaps you won't mind waiting till I get done, and then you can tell something of your own. We drew straws to decide who should sleep inside, and it fell to me. Such luck as that fellow Ben always had drawing straws when I held them! It was sinful! But even inside it was coldish, and I was more than an hour getting asleep. Toward morning, though, I woke, feeling very warm and peaceful. The moon was at full, just rising in the valley below, and, shining in at the hole I'd entered at, it made everything light as day."

"But, Sam, according to *my* astronomy a full moon never rises towards morning."

"Now, who said anything about your astronomy? I'd like to know who is telling this—you or I? Always think you know more than I do—and always swearing it isn't so—and always taking the words out of my mouth, and—but what's the use of arguing with *you*? As I was saying, the snakes began waking about the same time I did; I could hear them turn over on their other sides and sigh. Presently one raised himself up and yawned. He meant well, but it was not the regular thing for an ophidian to do at that season. By-and-by they began to poke their heads up all round, nodding good morning to one another across the room; and pretty soon one saw me lying there and called attention to the fact. Then they all began to crowd to the front and hang out over the sides of the beds in a fringe, to study my habits. I can't describe the strange spectacle: you would have supposed it was the middle of March and a forward season! There were more worms than I had counted, and they were larger ones than I had thought. And the more they got awake the wider they yawned, and the longer they stretched. The fat fellows in the hammocks above me were in danger of toppling out and breaking their necks every minute.

"Then it went through my mind like a flash what was the matter. Finding it cold outside, Ben had made a roaring fire on the top of the rock, and the heat had deceived the worms into the belief that it was late spring. As I lay there and thought of a full-grown man who hadn't any better sense than to do such a thing as *that*, I was mad enough to kill him. I lost confidence in mankind. If I had not stopped up the entrance before lying down, with a big round stone which the heat had swollen so that a hydraulic ram couldn't have butted it loose, I should have put on my clothes and gone straight home."

"But, Sam, you said the entrance was open, and the moon shining in."

"There you go again! Always contradicting—and insinuating that the moon must remain for hours in one position—and saying you've heard it told better by some one else—and wanting to fight! I've told this story to your brother over at Milk River more than a hundred million times, and he never said a word against it."

"I believe you, Samuel; for he is deaf as a tombstone."

"Tell you what to do for him! I know a fellow in Smith's Valley will cure him in a minute. That fellow has cleaned the deafness all out of Washington County a dozen times. I never knew a case of it that could stand up against him ten seconds. Take three parts of snake-root to a gallon of waggon-grease, and—I'll go and see if I can find the prescription!"

And Sam was off like a rocket.

MAUD'S PAPA

That is she in the old black silk—the one with the gimlet curls and the accelerated lap-cat. Doesn't she average about as I set her forth?

"Never told you anything about her?" Well, I will.

Twenty years ago, many a young man, of otherwise good character, would have ameliorated his condition for that girl; and would have thought himself overpaid if she had restored a fosy on his sepulchre. Maud would have been of the same opinion—and wouldn't have construed the fosy. And she was the most sagacious girl I ever experienced! As you shall hear.

I was her lover, and she was mine. We loved ourselves to detraction. Maud lived a mile from any other house—except one brick barn. Not even a watch-dog about the place—except her father. This pompous old weakling hated me boisterously; he said I was dedicated to hard drink, and when in that condition was perfectly incompatible. I did not like him, too.

One evening I called on Maud, and was surprised to meet her at the gate, with a shawl drawn over her head, and apparently in great combustion. She told me, hastily, the old man was ill of a fever, and had nearly derided her by going crazy.

This was all a lie; something had gone wrong with the old party's eyes—amanuensis of the equinox, or something; he couldn't see well, but he was no more crazy than I was sober.

"I was sitting quietly by him," said Maud, "when he sat up in bed and be-*gan!* You never in all your born life! I'm so glad you've come; you can take care of him while I fetch the doctor. He's quiet enough now, but you just wait till he gets another paralogism. When *they*'re on—oh my! You mustn't let him talk, nor get out of bed; doctor says it would prolong the diagnosis. Go right in, now. Oh dear! whatever shall I ought to do?"

And, blowing her eyes on the corner of her shawl, Maud shot away like a comic.

I walked hurriedly into the house, and entered the old man's dromedary, without knocking.

The playful girl had left that room a moment before, with every appearance of being frightened. She had told the old one there was a robber in the house, and the venerable invalid was a howling coward—I tell you this because I scorn to deceive you.

I found the old gentleman with his head under the blankets, very quiet and speaceful: but the moment he heard me he got up, and yelled like a heliotrope. Then he fixed on me a wild spiercing look from his bloodshot eyes, and for the first time in my life I believed Maud had told me the truth for the first time in hers. Then he reached out for a heavy cane. But I was too punctual for him, and, clapping my hand on his breast, I crowded him down, holding him tight. He curvetted some; then lay still, and swore weak oaths that wouldn't have hurt a sick chicken! All this time I was firm as a rock of amaranth. Presently, moreover, he spoke very low and resigned like— except his teeth chattered:

"Desperate man, there is no need; you will find it to the north-westcorner of my upper secretary drawer. I spromise not to appear."

"All right, my lobster-snouted bulbul," said I, delighted with the importunity of abusing him; "that is the dryest place you could keep it in, old spoolcotton! Be sure you don't let the light get to it, angleworm! Meantime, therefore, you must take this draught."

"Draught!" he shrieked, meandering from the subject. "O my poor child!"—and he sprang up again, screaming a multiple of things.

I had him by the shoulders in a minute, and crushed him back—except his legs kept agitating.

"Keep still, will you?" said I, "you sugarcoated old mandible, or I'll conciliate your exegesis with a proletarian!"

I never had such a flow of language in my life; I could say anything I wanted to.

He quailed at that threat, for, deleterious as I thought him, he saw I meant it; but he affected to prefer it that way to taking it out of the bottle.

"Better," he moaned, "better even that than the poison. Spare me the poisoned chalice, and you may do it in the way you mention."

The "draught," it may be sproper to explain, was comprised in a large bottle sitting on the table. I thought it was medicine— except it was black—and although Maud (sweet screature!) had not told me to give him anything, I felt sure this was nasty enough for him, or anybody. And it was; it was ink. So I treated his proposed compromise with silent contempt, merely remarking, as I uncorked the bottle: "Medicine's medicine, my fine friend; and it is for the sick." Then, spinioning his arms with one of mine, I concerted the neck of the bottle between his teeth.

"Now, you lacustrine old cylinder-escapement," I exclaimed, with some warmth, "hand up your stomach for this healing precoction, or I'm blest if I won't controvert your *raison d'etre!*"

He struggled hard, but, owing to my habit of finishing what I undertake, without any success. In ten minutes it was all down—except that some of it was spouted about rather circumstantially over the bedding, and walls, and me. There was more of the draught than I had thought. As he had been two days ill, I had supposed the bottle must be nearly empty; but, of course, when you think of it, a man doesn't abrogate much ink in an ordinary attack—except editors.

Just as I got my knees off the spatient's breast, Maud peeped in at the door. She had remained in the lane till she thought the charm had had time to hibernate, then came in to have her laugh. She began having it, gently; but seeing me with the empty bottle in my sable hand, and the murky inspiration rolling off my face in gasconades, she got graver, and came in very soberly.

Wherewith, the draught had done its duty, and the old gentleman was enjoying the first rest he had known since I came to heal him. He is enjoying it yet, for he was as dead as a monogram.

As there was a good deal of scandal about my killing a sprospective father-in-law, I had to live it down by not marrying Maud—who has lived single, as a rule, ever since. All this epigastric tercentenary might have been avoided if she had only allowed a good deal of margin for my probable condition when she splanned her little practicable joke.

"Why didn't they hang me?"—— Waiter, bring me a brandy spunch.—Well, that is the most didactic question! But if you must know—they did.

JIM BECKWOURTH'S POND

Not long after *that* (said old Jim Beckwourth, beginning a new
story) there was a party of about a dozen of us down in the
Powder River country, after buffalo. It was the *worst* place! Just
think of the most barren and sterile spot you ever saw, or ever
will see. Now take that spot and double it: that is where *we*
were. One day, about noon, we halted near a sickly little
arroyo, that was just damp enough to have deluded some feeble
bunches of bonnet-wire into setting up as grass along its banks.
After picketing the horses and pack-mules we took luncheon,
and then, while the others smoked and played cards for half-
dollars, I took my rifle and strolled off into the hills to see if I
could find a blind rabbit, or a lame antelope, that had been
unable to leave the country. As I went on I heard, at intervals
of about a quarter of an hour, a strange throbbing sound, as of
smothered thunder, which grew more distinct as I advanced.
Presently I came upon a lake of near a mile in diameter, and
almost circular. It was as calm and even as a mirror, but I
could see by a light steamy haze above it that the water was
nearly at boiling heat—a not very uncommon circumstance in
that region. While I looked, big bubbles began to rise to the
surface, chase one another about, and burst; and suddenly,
without any other preliminary movement, there occurred the
most awful and astounding event that (with a single exception)
it has ever been my lot to witness! I stood rooted to the spot
with horror, and when it was all over, and again the lake lay
smiling placidly before me, I silently thanked Heaven I had
been standing at some distance from the deceitful pool. In a
quarter of an hour the frightful scene was repeated, preceded as

before by the rising and bursting of bubbles, and producing in me the utmost terror; but after seeing it three or four times I became calm. Then I went back to camp, and told the boys there was a tolerably interesting pond near by, if they cared for such things.

At first they did not, but when I had thrown in a few lies about the brilliant hues of the water, and the great number of swans, they laid down their cards, left Lame Dave to look after the horses, and followed me back to see. Just before we crossed the last range of hills we heard a thundering sound ahead, which somewhat astonished the boys, but I said nothing till we stood on a low knoll overlooking the lake. There it lay, as peaceful as a dead Indian, of a dull grey colour, and as innocent of water-fowl as a new-born babe.

"There!" said I, triumphantly, pointing to it.

"Well," said Bill Buckster, leaning on his rifle and surveying it critically, "what's the matter with the pond? I don't see nothin' in *that* puddle."

"Whar's yer swans?" asked Gus Jamison.

"And yer prismatic warter?" added Stumpy Jack.

"Well, I like *this!*" drawled Frenchwoman Pete. "What 'n thunder d' ye mean, you derned saddle-coloured fraud?"

I was a little nettled at all this, particularly as the lake seemed to have buried the hatchet for that day; but I thought I would "cheek it through."

"Just you wait!" I replied, significantly.

"O yes!" exclaimed Stumpy, derisively; "'course, boys, you mus' *wait*. 'Tain't no use a-hurryin' up the cattle; yer mustn't rush the buck. Jest wait till some feller comes along with a melted rainbow, and lays on the war-paint! and another feller

Ambrose Bierce

fetches the swans' eggs, and sets on 'em, and hatches 'em out!—and me a-holding both bowers an' the ace!" he added, regretfully, thinking of the certainty he had left, to follow a delusive hope.

Then I pointed out to them a wide margin of wet and steaming clay surrounding the water on all sides, asking them if *that* wasn't worth coming to see.

"*That!*" exclaimed Gus. "I've seen the same thing a thousand million times! It's the reg'lar thing in Idaho. Clay soaks up the water and sweats it out."

To verify his theory he started away, down to the shore. I was concerned for Gus, but I did not dare call him back for fear of betraying my secret in some way. Besides, I knew he would not come; and he ought not to have been so sceptical, anyhow.

Just then two or three big bubbles rose to the surface, and silently exploded. Quick as lightning I dropped on my knees and raised my arms.

"Now may Heaven grant my prayer," I began with awful solemnity, "and send the great Ranunculus to loose the binding chain of concupiscence, heaving the multitudinous aquacity upon the heads of this wicked and sententious generation, whelming these diametrical scoffers in a supercilious Constantinople!"

I knew the long words would impress their simple souls with a belief that I was actually praying; and I was right, for every man of them pulled his hat off, and stood staring at me with a mixed look of reverence, incredulity, and astonishment—but not for long. For before I could say amen, yours truly, or anything, that entire body of water shot upward five hundred feet into the air, as smooth as a column of crystal, curled over in broad green cataracts, falling outward with a jar and thunder like the explosion of a thousand subterranean cannon, then surging and swirling back to the centre, one steaming, writing mass of snowy foam!

As I rose to my feet to put my hand in my pocket for a chew of tobacco, I looked complacently about upon my comrades. Stumpy Jack stood paralysed, his head thrown back at an alarming angle, precisely as he had tilted it to watch the ascending column, and his neck somehow out of joint, holding it there. All the others were down upon their marrow-bones, white with terror, praying with extraordinary fervency, each trying his best to master the ridiculous jargon they had heard me use, but employing it with an even greater disregard of sense and fitness than I did. Away over on the next range of hills, toward camp, was something that looked like a giant spider, scrambling up the steep side of the sand-hill, and sliding down a trifle faster than it got up. It was Lame Dave, who had abandoned his equine trust, to come up at the eleventh hour and see the swans. He had seen enough, and was now trying, in his weak way, to get back to camp.

In a few minutes I had got Stumpy's head back into the position assigned it by Nature, had crowded his eyes in, and was going about with a reassuring smile, helping the pious upon their feet. Not a word was spoken; I took the lead, and we strode solemnly to camp, picking up Lame Dave at the foot of his acclivity, played a little game for Gus Jamison's horse and "calamities," then mounted our steeds, departing thence. Three or four days afterward I ventured cautiously upon a covert allusion to peculiar lakes, but the simultaneous clicking of ten revolvers convinced me that I need not trouble myself to pursue the subject.

STRINGING A BEAR

"I was looking for my horse one morning, up in the San Joaquin Valley," said old Sandy Fowler, absently stirring the camp fire, "when I saw a big bull grizzly lying in the sunshine, picking his teeth with his claws, and smiling, as if he said, 'You need not mind the horse, old fellow; he's been found.' I at once gave a loud whoop, which I thought would be heard by the boys in the camp, and prepared to string the brute."

"Oh, I know how it goes," interrupted Smarty Mellor, as we called him; "seen it done heaps o' times! Six or eight o' ye rides up to the b'ar, and s'rounds him, every son-of-a-gun with a *riata* a mile long, and worries him till he gits his mad up, and while he's a-chasin' one feller the others is a-goin' aeter him, and a-floorin' of him by loopin' his feet as they comes up behind, and when he turns onto them fellers the other chappy turns onto him, and puts another loop onto his feet as they comes up behind, and then—"

"I bound my *riata* tightly about my wrist," resumed old Sandy, composedly, "so that the beast should not jerk away when I had got him. Then I advanced upon him—very slowly, so as not to frighten him away. Seeing me coming, he rose upon his haunches, to have a look at me. He was about the size of a house—say a small two-storey house, with a Mansard roof. I paused a moment, to take another turn of the thong about my wrist.

"Again I moved obliquely forward, trying to look as if I were thinking about the new waterworks in San Francisco, or the next presidential election, so as not to frighten him away. The brute now rose squarely upon end, with his paws suspended before him, like a dog begging for a biscuit, and I thought what a very large biscuit he must be begging for! Halting a moment, to see if the *riata* was likely to cut into my wrist, I perceived the beast had an inkling of my design, and was trying stupidly to stretch his head up out of reach.

"I now threw off all disguise, and whirled my cord with a wide circular sweep, and in another moment it would have been very unpleasant for Bruin, but somehow the line appeared to get foul. While I was opening the noose, the animal settled upon his feet and came toward me; but the moment he saw me begin to whirl again, he got frightened, up-ended himself as before, and shut his eyes.

"Then I felt in my belt to see if my knife was there, when the bear got down again and came forward, utterly regardless.

"Seeing he was frightened and trying to escape by coming so close I could not have a fair fling at him, I dropped the noose on the ground and walked away, trailing the line behind me. When it was all run out, the rascal arrived at the loop. He first smelled it, then opened it with his paws, and putting it about his neck, tilted up again, and nodded significantly.

"I pulled out my knife, and severing the line at my wrist, walked away, looking for some one to introduce me to Smarty Mellor."

Ambrose Bierce

Choose from Thousands of 1stWorldLibrary Classics By

A. M. Barnard	Booth Tarkington	Edward Everett Hale
Ada Leverson	Boyd Cable	Edward J. O'Biren
Adolphus William Ward	Bram Stoker	Edward S. Ellis
Aesop	C. Collodi	Edwin L. Arnold
Agatha Christie	C. E. Orr	Eleanor Atkins
Alexander Aaronsohn	C. M. Ingleby	Eleanor Hallowell Abbott
Alexander Kielland	Carolyn Wells	Eliot Gregory
Alexandre Dumas	Catherine Parr Traill	Elizabeth Gaskell
Alfred Gatty	Charles A. Eastman	Elizabeth McCracken
Alfred Ollivant	Charles Amory Beach	Elizabeth Von Arnim
Alice Duer Miller	Charles Dickens	Ellem Key
Alice Turner Curtis	Charles Dudley Warner	Emerson Hough
Alice Dunbar	Charles Farrar Browne	Emilie F. Carlen
Allen Chapman	Charles Ives	Emily Bronte
Alleyne Ireland	Charles Kingsley	Emily Dickinson
Ambrose Bierce	Charles Klein	Enid Bagnold
Amelia E. Barr	Charles Hanson Towne	Enilor Macartney Lane
Amory H. Bradford	Charles Lathrop Pack	Erasmus W. Jones
Andrew Lang	Charles Romyn Dake	Ernie Howard Pie
Andrew McFarland Davis	Charles Whibley	Ethel May Dell
Andy Adams	Charles Willing Beale	Ethel Turner
Angela Brazil	Charlotte M. Braeme	Ethel Watts Mumford
Anna Alice Chapin	Charlotte M. Yonge	Eugene Sue
Anna Sewell	Charlotte Perkins Stetson	Eugenie Foa
Annie Besant	Clair W. Hayes	Eugene Wood
Annie Hamilton Donnell	Clarence Day Jr.	Eustace Hale Ball
Annie Payson Call	Clarence E. Mulford	Evelyn Everett-green
Annie Roe Carr	Clemence Housman	Everard Cotes
Annonaymous	Confucius	F. H. Cheley
Anton Chekhov	Coningsby Dawson	F. J. Cross
Archibald Lee Fletcher	Cornelis DeWitt Wilcox	F. Marion Crawford
Arnold Bennett	Cyril Burleigh	Fannie E. Newberry
Arthur C. Benson	D. H. Lawrence	Federick Austin Ogg
Arthur Conan Doyle	Daniel Defoe	Ferdinand Ossendowski
Arthur M. Winfield	David Garnett	Fergus Hume
Arthur Ransome	Dinah Craik	Florence A. Kilpatrick
Arthur Schnitzler	Don Carlos Janes	Fremont B. Deering
Arthur Train	Donald Keyhoe	Francis Bacon
Atticus	Dorothy Kilner	Francis Darwin
B.H. Baden-Powell	Dougan Clark	Frances Hodgson Burnett
B. M. Bower	Douglas Fairbanks	Frances Parkinson Keyes
B. C. Chatterjee	E. Nesbit	Frank Gee Patchin
Baroness Emmuska Orczy	E. P. Roe	Frank Harris
Baroness Orczy	E. Phillips Oppenheim	Frank Jewett Mather
Basil King	E. S. Brooks	Frank L. Packard
Bayard Taylor	Earl Barnes	Frank V. Webster
Ben Macomber	Edgar Rice Burroughs	Frederic Stewart Isham
Bertha Muzzy Bower	Edith Van Dyne	Frederick Trevor Hill
Bjornstjerne Bjornson	Edith Wharton	Frederick Winslow Taylor

Friedrich Kerst
Friedrich Nietzsche
Fyodor Dostoyevsky
G.A. Henty
G.K. Chesterton
Gabrielle E. Jackson
Garrett P. Serviss
Gaston Leroux
George A. Warren
George Ade
Geroge Bernard Shaw
George Cary Eggleston
George Durston
George Ebers
George Eliot
George Gissing
George MacDonald
George Meredith
George Orwell
George Sylvester Viereck
George Tucker
George W. Cable
George Wharton James
Gertrude Atherton
Gordon Casserly
Grace E. King
Grace Gallatin
Grace Greenwood
Grant Allen
Guillermo A. Sherwell
Gulielma Zollinger
Gustav Flaubert
H. A. Cody
H. B. Irving
H.C. Bailey
H. G. Wells
H. H. Munro
H. Irving Hancock
H. R. Naylor
H. Rider Haggard
H. W. C. Davis
Haldeman Julius
Hall Caine
Hamilton Wright Mabie
Hans Christian Andersen
Harold Avery
Harold McGrath
Harriet Beecher Stowe
Harry Castlemon
Harry Coghill
Harry Houidini

Hayden Carruth
Helent Hunt Jackson
Helen Nicolay
Hendrik Conscience
Hendy David Thoreau
Henri Barbusse
Henrik Ibsen
Henry Adams
Henry Ford
Henry Frost
Henry James
Henry Jones Ford
Henry Seton Merriman
Henry W Longfellow
Herbert A. Giles
Herbert Carter
Herbert N. Casson
Herman Hesse
Hildegard G. Frey
Homer
Honore De Balzac
Horace B. Day
Horace Walpole
Horatio Alger Jr.
Howard Pyle
Howard R. Garis
Hugh Lofting
Hugh Walpole
Humphry Ward
Ian Maclaren
Inez Haynes Gillmore
Irving Bacheller
Isabel Cecilia Williams
Isabel Hornibrook
Israel Abrahams
Ivan Turgenev
J.G.Austin
J. Henri Fabre
J. M. Barrie
J. M. Walsh
J. Macdonald Oxley
J. R. Miller
J. S. Fletcher
J. S. Knowles
J. Storer Clouston
J. W. Duffield
Jack London
Jacob Abbott
James Allen
James Andrews
James Baldwin

James Branch Cabell
James DeMille
James Joyce
James Lane Allen
James Lane Allen
James Oliver Curwood
James Oppenheim
James Otis
James R. Driscoll
Jane Abbott
Jane Austen
Jane L. Stewart
Janet Aldridge
Jens Peter Jacobsen
Jerome K. Jerome
Jessie Graham Flower
John Buchan
John Burroughs
John Cournos
John F. Kennedy
John Gay
John Glasworthy
John Habberton
John Joy Bell
John Kendrick Bangs
John Milton
John Philip Sousa
John Taintor Foote
Jonas Lauritz Idemil Lie
Jonathan Swift
Joseph A. Altsheler
Joseph Carey
Joseph Conrad
Joseph E. Badger Jr
Joseph Hergesheimer
Joseph Jacobs
Jules Vernes
Julian Hawthrone
Julie A Lippmann
Justin Huntly McCarthy
Kakuzo Okakura
Karle Wilson Baker
Kate Chopin
Kenneth Grahame
Kenneth McGaffey
Kate Langley Bosher
Kate Langley Bosher
Katherine Cecil Thurston
Katherine Stokes
L. A. Abbot
L. T. Meade

L. Frank Baum
Latta Griswold
Laura Dent Crane
Laura Lee Hope
Laurence Housman
Lawrence Beasley
Leo Tolstoy
Leonid Andreyev
Lewis Carroll
Lewis Sperry Chafer
Lilian Bell
Lloyd Osbourne
Louis Hughes
Louis Joseph Vance
Louis Tracy
Louisa May Alcott
Lucy Fitch Perkins
Lucy Maud Montgomery
Luther Benson
Lydia Miller Middleton
Lyndon Orr
M. Corvus
M. H. Adams
Margaret E. Sangster
Margret Howth
Margaret Vandercook
Margaret W. Hungerford
Margret Penrose
Maria Edgeworth
Maria Thompson Daviess
Mariano Azuela
Marion Polk Angellotti
Mark Overton
Mark Twain
Mary Austin
Mary Catherine Crowley
Mary Cole
Mary Hastings Bradley
Mary Roberts Rinehart
Mary Rowlandson
M. Wollstonecraft Shelley
Maud Lindsay
Max Beerbohm
Myra Kelly
Nathaniel Hawthrone
Nicolo Machiavelli
O. F. Walton
Oscar Wilde
Owen Johnson
P.G. Wodehouse
Paul and Mabel Thorne

Paul G. Tomlinson
Paul Severing
Percy Brebner
Percy Keese Fitzhugh
Peter B. Kyne
Plato
Quincy Allen
R. Derby Holmes
R. L. Stevenson
R. S. Ball
Rabindranath Tagore
Rahul Alvares
Ralph Bonehill
Ralph Henry Barbour
Ralph Victor
Ralph Waldo Emmerson
Rene Descartes
Ray Cummings
Rex Beach
Rex E. Beach
Richard Harding Davis
Richard Jefferies
Richard Le Gallienne
Robert Barr
Robert Frost
Robert Gordon Anderson
Robert L. Drake
Robert Lansing
Robert Lynd
Robert Michael Ballantyne
Robert W. Chambers
Rosa Nouchette Carey
Rudyard Kipling
Saint Augustine
Samuel B. Allison
Samuel Hopkins Adams
Sarah Bernhardt
Sarah C. Hallowell
Selma Lagerlof
Sherwood Anderson
Sigmund Freud
Standish O'Grady
Stanley Weyman
Stella Benson
Stella M. Francis
Stephen Crane
Stewart Edward White
Stijn Streuvels
Swami Abhedananda
Swami Parmananda
T. S. Ackland

T. S. Arthur
The Princess Der Ling
Thomas A. Janvier
Thomas A Kempis
Thomas Anderton
Thomas Bailey Aldrich
Thomas Bulfinch
Thomas De Quincey
Thomas Dixon
Thomas H. Huxley
Thomas Hardy
Thomas More
Thornton W. Burgess
U. S. Grant
Upton Sinclair
Valentine Williams
Various Authors
Vaughan Kester
Victor Appleton
Victor G. Durham
Victoria Cross
Virginia Woolf
Wadsworth Camp
Walter Camp
Walter Scott
Washington Irving
Wilbur Lawton
Wilkie Collins
Willa Cather
Willard F. Baker
William Dean Howells
William le Queux
W. Makepeace Thackeray
William W. Walter
William Shakespeare
Winston Churchill
Yei Theodora Ozaki
Yogi Ramacharaka
Young E. Allison
Zane Grey

www.ingramcontent.com/pod-product-compliance
Lightning Source LLC
Chambersburg PA
CBHW030118180626
46812CB00002B/466